L. C Corbett, Jean d'Artigue

Six Years in the Canadian North-West

L. C Corbett, Jean d'Artigue

Six Years in the Canadian North-West

ISBN/EAN: 9783337188740

Printed in Europe, USA, Canada, Australia, Japan

Cover: Foto ©Andreas Hilbeck / pixelio.de

More available books at **www.hansebooks.com**

SIX YEARS

IN

THE CANADIAN NORTH-WEST.

BY

MONS. JEAN D'ARTIGUE.

Translated from the French by L. C. Corbett, Esq., B. A., and Rev. S. Smith, B.D.

Toronto:
HUNTER, ROSE AND COMPANY.
1882.

PREFACE.

THIS Book, which I dedicate to the Canadian Public,
is not a work of fiction, but is purely historical.
In writing it, elegance of style has not been studied, but
rather a simple relation of facts as they occur. It may
be wanting in interest to the lover of imaginary adventure, but to those who love the truth, I trust it will be
found sufficiently interesting to repay a perusal.

My object in undertaking this work is not to gain
notoriety, but to furnish the Canadian Public with an
account, not yet given by any writer, of the object of the
organization of the North-West Mounted Police Force,
the trials, privations, and adventures which they encountered, and the results of the expedition.

This book is divided into three parts, the first of which
contains a history of the campaign of the North-West
Mounted Police, in the year 1874, under command of
Colonel French, and though it is short, it relates facts
which should form a few pages of Canadian history and

being an eye-witness, I have simply stated the facts, leaving to the general public the task of deducing conclusions.

The second part contains the history of our sojourn in the far North-West, and gives an account of the journeys made by myself over vast plains; the first, undertaken to acquaint myself with the manners and actions of the Indians in their primeval state, and the second, in discharge of official duty, and to study further the Indian character.

The third part is an account of my return journey from Fort Saskatchewan *via* Saskatchewan and Red River, and Lakes Winnepeg, Superior, and Huron to Sarnia, and thence by rail to Quebec. This part will be found the most interesting of the three, and also the most useful to intending settlers in the North-West as it contains geographical and agricultural information which will give an idea of the future of that region traversed by the Saskatchewan.

CHAPTER VI.

CHAPTER VII.

CHAPTER VIII.

CHAPTER IX.

CHAPTER X.

SIX YEARS

IN THE

CANADIAN NORTH-WEST.

CHAPTER I.

General State of Affairs in the North-West Territories previous to the year
1874—Organization of the North-West Mounted Police Force—My
Enlistment in that Corps—The Apostle of Temperance—Military Life
during our Stay at the New Fort of Toronto.

QUITE recently on the vast plains watered by the
Missouri and the Saskatchewan rivers, numerous
herds of buffaloes roamed, whose hides were eagerly
sought for by fur-traders. Some of these fur-traders, taking
advantage of the craving appetite for strong drinks which
characterises the Indian race, made a practice of exchang-
ing liquor for furs, and thus obtained them at a price
very much less than their market value. The result of
such dishonest transactions was often disastrous : for
the Indians, once under the influence of alcohol, are
transformed into wild beasts, and having obtained a
quantity of it, they would keep themselves under its in-

fluence as long as the supply lasted. While in this state
they would fall unexpectedly upon the fur-traders and
colonists whom they massacred without mercy; and, not
contented with this inhuman slaughter of the whites,
they were continually at war among themselves. Such
was the state of affairs in the North-West Territories at the time of their annexation to the Dominion of
Canada.

To put an end to this, and, at the same time, to prevent
the total destruction of the buffaloes, which were hunted
almost solely for their hides, the Dominion Parliament
passed laws prohibiting the manufacture and importation
of alcoholic liquors into the above country. But this did
not stay the odious traffic, nor did it prevent the massacres (which, for the most part, were perpetrated in the
neighbourhood of the Rocky Mountains and remained
unpunished). Therefore, in the year 1873, the Government,
under the leadership of Sir John A. Macdonald, resolved to
organize a Mounted Police Force, to send to the North-
West, whose presence there, it was thought, would have a
salutary effect upon both the fur-traders and the Indians.
This corps, composed exclusively of volunteers, numbered
300 horsemen, called constables and sub-constables, and
was divided into six divisions, each commanded by an Inspector, assisted by two sub-Inspectors. At the head of
the whole force was placed a Commissioner and an Assist-
ant-Commissioner. With this handful of men, the Government expected to restore order in the North-West

Territories. We will see later on, to what extent this force fulfilled the expectations of the Government.

In April, 1874, I was in Montreal, and, one morning opening the *Witness*, my attention was directed to an advertisement, the substance of which ran as follows :

"The Dominion Government requires 150 volunteers for the North-West Mounted Police. The knowledge of English or French is obligatory. Moreover, the candidate must have good antecedents, and be a good horseman. For further particulars, apply to Colonel Bacon.

"A. FRENCH,

"*Commissioner.*"

Not knowing what portion of the Dominion was called the North-West, nor the nature of the duties of the Mounted Police, I at once called on a friend, showed him the advertisement, and asked him what it meant. This gentleman, thoroughly versed in Canadian affairs, acquainted me with the fact, that by the North-West was meant all that tract of country which is bounded on the west by the Rocky Mountains ; on the south, by the United States ; on the east, by the Provinces of Ontario and Quebec, and the Atlantic Ocean ; and on the north, by the Polar Seas. He dwelt largely on the natural richness of this vast territory, which the building of the Canadian Pacific Railway would place within the reach of millions of homeless people. He also said that, in September of the previous year, three divisions of the North-West Mounted Police had left for Stone Fort, Manitoba; and with the 150 volunteers advertised for here, three more

divisions were to be organised at Toronto. He said further, that, in the following summer, this police force would
make an expedition among the Indian tribes of the North-
West, in order to stop, if possible, the liquor traffic that
American traders were carrying on in our territories. My
friend carefully pointed out the difficulties and dangers
which this expedition would encounter, and said, in conclusion, that if everybody knew as much as he did about
the North-West, the Government would not easily find
300 men who would thus run the risk of losing their
scalps.

On my way back to my lodgings, I began to ponder
on the last words of my friend, the word "scalp" rousing
in my mind scenes that I had quite forgotten. In my
younger days, the works of Fenimore Cooper, and other
novel writers had impressed me with a desire to visit
those countries, whose inhabitants could perform such
wonderful feats, and I rejoiced that now it was in my
power to satisfy my curiosity ; all I had to do was to enlist in the North-West Mounted Police Force. So I at
once called on Colonel Bacon who, after perusing my certificates of age, character, education and nationality,
wrote me down as a candidate. He told me to present
myself at the military barracks, on the 14th instant, when
Colonel French would be present for the purpose of test-
ing and enlisting men, and he had no doubt I would be
accepted.

Accordingly, on the day appointed, I presented myself
at the barracks, which I found surrounded by a large

crowd, most of them candidates for enlistment like myself. Everyone was provided with certificates from men of high standing, both in the government and in the church; and being a foreigner, I expected to be rejected. I was, therefore, greatly surprised when, with a few more, I was selected to pass the doctor's final examination for enlistment. Passing this, no words can express the happiness I felt when told I was accepted, and to be at the Grand Trunk Railway station on the evening of the 16th inst., where we would take the train for Toronto.

On returning home, I began my preparations for departure, speculating the while on the novelties and excitement of my future life. I fancied I saw myself, with some of my comrades riding days and nights together, over the vast plains of the North-West, fighting the Indians and the whiskey traders. I saw settlements destroyed by the red man, the ladies carried away to worse than slavery; husbands and fathers calling upon us to rescue their wives and daughters; ourselves rushing immediately to horse, and over the plains *péle méle*, in hot pursuit; and, after a long day's ride, coming upon the Indians at night, when a brief but fierce struggle would ensue and we would rescue the captives, and carry them back in triumph to their desolated homes.

With such exciting fancies floating through my mind, I again visited my friend and said: "Well, Mr. C., I start the day after to-morrow for Toronto." "For Toronto?" said he. "Yes," said I, "I have enlisted in the North-West Mounted Police force." "Ha, ha," said he, "tell

that to those that don't know you.   One don't give up
an advantageous career like yours, to embrace an adventurous one."   "You don't believe me," said I, "come to
the railway station to-morrow night, and you will see."

Seeing that I was in earnest, he then tried to dissuade
me from following up my projects ; stating, in eloquent
and earnest language, the folly of giving up teaching for
a life of adventure.   I let him talk for an hour without
interruption, and I am sure his reasons and arguments
were good.   But with my Quixotic ideas, and my young
imagination of twenty years, I could only see fights, sieges,
and victories.

As arranged by the Commissioner, on the evening of
the 16th, after bidding good-bye to my friends, I went to
the G. T. Railway station where I found some of the new
members of the North-West Mounted Police had preceded
me.   The time for starting having arrived, we were soon
on the way to Toronto.

In the car, sitting opposite me, was a traveller, appar-
ently about thirty years of age, whose dress would indicate the clergyman : long black coat, waistcoat buttoned
to the chin, straight collar, and broad brimmed hat ; and
yet, his piercing eye, his *moustache à l'impériale*, and his
martial appearance, told me that I was facing a soldier.

Feeling somewhat lonely, and in order to make the
time pass quickly, I entered into conversation with my
neighbour by asking him in a true Yankee style : "Where
are you going sir ?"   "To Toronto," said he, "to join the
North-West Mounted Police,—a military corps, organised

for the purpose of putting an end to the liquor traffic in that country. I am an apostle of temperance, sir, my whole life is consecrated to that cause."

If all the members of the force are like this one, thought I, the whiskey traders will do well to decamp before our arrival. For my part, being accustomed to, and fond of, good wine, I did not share the opinions of my fellow traveller, who went on discussing the injurious effects of alcohol, and condemning even our best French wines. This was more than a Frenchman likes to bear, and I was about to give him a piece of my mind, when the conductor called out "Prescott." My attention was immediately directed to three young men, who entered the car, each one bearing a small parcel. "I don't think there is anyone here for the M. Police," said one of them glancing all around. "Here is one," said the apostle of temperance, "and one that will count." So saying, he left me and joined the newcomers.

As he before had done with me, he spoke lengthily and in parsonical style of the duties which would devolve upon the volunteers. "Hold on, old fellow," said one after a while, taking out a bottle, "here is the kind of beverage that would be of service to us in the coming expedition. Have a swig, you must be dry after so long a speech." Thus addressed, the apostle was filled with astonishment and horror. "Is it possible," said he, "that you expect with vice to correct vice," and leaving them, he returned to his former seat. I could now see that not only total abstainers were being enlisted, but also those who were fond of their glass.

About day-light we reached the City of Toronto, and proceeded towards the New Fort where we were to be quartered, until the whole force was made up.

We had been preceded there by about thirty men, who were drilling on foot preparatory to horseback drill. As we drew near the fort, one of the constables came to us, showed us to a large room, and told us to make ourselves comfortable. I did not see how this could be done; for all I could see as furniture was a large table in the centre of the room. I did not, for a moment, expect that this would be our sleeping quarters, until we were called out to get from the store a straw mattress and two blankets each. This looked very much like military life, and yet, we saw at the door an order, reminding us that we were not soldiers, but civilians.

The next morning we joined the others at foot drill, and in a short time, made good progress, after which the riding drill began in the *manege*. I must say here, that most of us had overrated our proficiency in horsemanship; for when we came to ride without stirrups, many laughable falls ensued: men having lost their balance would cling to their horses in every imaginable position, till the drill-instructor coming up, would give the horse a smart lash with the whip, which would make him rear and plunge, till, freeing himself from his rider, he would gallop away to the stable. Even the officers were most of them as bad as ourselves at riding, but managed by some

means, unknown to us, to get out of the *manege* drill,
and went only to the field drill, where stirrups were allowed to be used. The Commissioner himself was a
thoroughly well drilled officer ; but most of the inspectors
and sub-inspectors did not understand the simplest field
manœuvres ; and their inefficiency was made manifest
before we left Toronto, by the three divisions being
called out together, when the Commissioner gave the first,
or general commands, which should have been followed
by others from the officers ; but their efforts almost invariably proved failures, and produced indescribable confusion. Fortunately we had some of the sergeants from
the regular army among us, who, on such occasions would
come forward, put the officers in their proper places and
restore us to order.

In the latter part of May, the organisation, training
and equipment of the three divisions were complete ; and
about the same time, the Commissioner received very serious tidings from the North-West. It was said that the
whiskey-traders were building fortifications, and inducing
the Indians to resist our approach. As energetic and resolute men could alone bring the projected expedition to a
successful issue, Colonel French called a general parade,
and, after making us acquainted with the above news, he
reminded us of the fact, that we were but volunteers, and
that, before going any farther, we should consider the
dangers and hardships we must necessarily encounter.
That on some occasions, we might be two or three days
without food, and have to camp in the open prairie, hav-

ing nothing but the canopy of heaven for covering. He ended by advising any of those who repented having enlisted to leave the ranks, and return to their homes.

Very few availed themselves of the opportunity; and this shows of what stamp of men the Mounted Police was composed. It is true they were not well trained, like regular soldiers, but certainly, courage and patriotism, qualities which every true soldier must possess, were not wanting in them.

CHAPTER II.

ON the first day of June, we took the oath of office
and the three following days were devoted in
carrying to the Grand Trunk Station, our equipments,
which were to be transported by rail as far as Fargo,
Dacotah. On the fifth we had a holiday. Finally on
the sixth, at 11 a.m., we started for the Railway Station with our horses. Our force was composed altogether
of 217 men and 244 horses. Two trains were in readiness for our reception, and, placing the horses in the cars
prepared for them, we went to the dining room of the
station where a substantial dinner had been prepared for
us. Thousands of people were surrounding the station.
One would have thought that all the inhabitants of the
city had made that their *rendezvous*.

Between the dinner and the departure, a music band
played a good selection of patriotic airs, reminding us of
the services that the country expected from us. On every
side, we were surrounded by an anxious crowd, each one
wishing to shake hands with us once more. The hour of

separation came at last. The train, which was to take
one division and a half, was waiting. Final words were
uttered : " you will write, will you not " said a mother
in tears to her son. " My son," said an old man, " remember your life belongs to the country. I would rather
hear of your death than of your dishonour." " Don't forget your dearest Angelica when you are among the Indians," added a young girl to her betrothed. And amid a
very Babel of such expressions we entered our train.

Most of the men were in good spirits, but doubtlessly
they would have been less so, if they had followed the
maxims of the " Apostle of Temperance" above mentioned.
Among us were some very good singers, and, when the
trains were starting, while the band played the Canadian National Anthem : " Vive la Canadienne,", they
sang : " The girl I left behind me."

Toronto was soon far behind us ; but the tokens of
sympathy were to follow us, not only through Ontario,
but also through the United States. At the windows of
the houses near the track, many were seen (specially
ladies, bless their sympathizing hearts) waving their
handkerchiefs as long as we remained in view. I understood then that beautiful device : " Fight for God, the
King and your Lady" which ever fills the breast of every
true Knight. By those signs, the ladies not only bade us
farewell, but reminded us to protect and love, in any
country where we went, the greatest earthly consolation
of man, the fair sex.

The next morning, at day-break the second train in

which I was (the first being several miles before us,) entered Sarnia (Pt. Edward). This town occupies an advantageous site on Lake Huron, at the head of St. Clair River, and from which port several lines of steamers plough the waters, not only of Lake Huron, but of the whole chain of lakes with which it is connected. Furthermore Sarnia is connected with the different commercial centres of Ontario and Quebec by two lines of railway, the Great Western and the Grand Trunk.

After taking a hearty meal at the station, we set out again on our journey, and crossing the St. Clair river by ferry, we entered the State of Michigan. The progress made by this state, during the last thirty years, is certainly wonderful. Passing rapidly over the country, and catching hurried views of the rich fields of wheat, the neat and comfortable cottages, surrounded by large orchards of various kinds of fruit, my mind went back to the time when that region was covered with dense forests, and the possession of which by the white man was obtained after many bloody battles with the Indians, the original and lawful owners. The wigwams are no more to be seen, and the plough, which carries civilisation with it, has taken the place of the tomahawk and the scalping knife of the savage.

During the previous night, the excitement was so great that we were unable to take any rest; so sleep came to claim her rights, and before long, our car looked like a dormitory. All were sleeping but myself and one other, a sub-constable of melancholy and taciturn appearance, who seemed disposed to remain awake. He was from Switzerland, speaking French; and wishing to know the reasons that induced such a man to enlist in the Mounted Police corps, I went over to him and addressed him in the following and familiar style; "comrade, what do you think of this beautiful country? I never saw anything like it." "Do you really think so?" said he, staring at me in surprise. "Why," said I, "look at those beautiful fields, those elegant houses surrounded by pretty gardens and parterres, really it is an Eden!" "What you wonder at and admire, I detest," said he, "I would not for worlds live in this country that you seem to think without an equal; for under the appearance of rich fields and beautiful houses, are hidden vices which undermine every society. The country that I would cherish, is one that would show no vestige of civilisation." "Such a land," I replied, "you will find in the North-West Territories, and yet, if we succeed in restoring peace and order in that part of the world, civilisation will soon reach it." "I hope not," said he, "but to avoid it reaching *me*, I intend, as soon as we reach Manitoba, to ask for my discharge, when I will marry an Indian woman, and settle down in a region entirely savage." "I see you are not only a countryman of the Swiss philosopher, Jean Jacques Rousseau," said I, "but also his disciple. As he did, you think the uncivilised man is, in many respects, superior to the civilised, and admitting for argument's sake that it is so, don't you see that in a few years those wild North-West Territories will be settled by colonists?" "If that

should happen," said he, "I will shift my quarters farther, even to the midst of the Rocky Mountains, if
necessary; and now, that you know my projects, keep
them to yourself."

I went back to my former seat, wondering why a man
imbued with such ideas had been selected for the Mounted
Police Corps. I never thought that in our time there
were men who shared the paradoxical opinions of the
Swiss philosopher. For my part, I never could see in
what respect the uncivilised man was superior to the
civilised.

Like the rest of my companions, I soon went to sleep,
and never awoke until I heard some of the train-men
shouting "Chicago!" It was ten o'clock at night. First
of all, we took out the horses, placed them in an enclosure
near the station, and watered and fed them. This done,
the roll was called, and a certain number of us selected,
in alphabetical order, for night watch, and those who were
not on duty went into the city, to enjoy once more the
comforts of civilisation.

Chicago, which is situated on the southern shore of
Lake Michigan, is the most important city in the northern
States. Some fifty years ago it was but a hamlet, composed of a few log-houses; but, at the present time, it has
a population of about 630,000 souls. The industry and
commerce of this city are very extensive. Its docks receive
a great quantity of grain from Dacotah and Minnesota for
exportation to European markets. Its slaughter-houses
are very numerous, from which are shipped immense

quantities of beef and pork; and, in regard to buildings, very few cities in the United States rank as high as Chicago.

During our journey from Toronto to Fargo, the Government allowed each man a dollar per diem, to cover his boarding expenses. Through Ontario and Michigan this allowance was quite sufficient, as the Commissioner, before we left Toronto, had made arrangements with different railway stations to have meals ready for us at 25c. per man. But in Chicago, no arrangement of that sort had been made; there we had to pay 50c. for every meal we took: hence a good deal of grumbling on our part against the Yankees. But, happily, our stay there was very short; for in the afternoon of the next day, we started again on our journey. Passing along the shore of Lake Michigan, we reached Milwaukee, the capital of the State of Wisconsin. Remaining there but a short time, we were soon on our way to St. Paul, which we reached after a journey of one day and two nights from Chicago.

St. Paul is not such a flourishing city as Chicago, but its inhabitants are more hospitable; and in our friendly intercourse with them, they were even too much so; for they tried to persuade us to give up our expedition and remain with them. Among other arguments used, they stated that the American posts, established on Indian territories numbered several thousand men: yet, these posts were often attacked and the men massacred. We replied that we were not afraid; and that they must not forget, that a Canadian fighting under the British flag, considers himself equal to three or four Yankees.

The next day in the afternoon, we left St. Paul by the Northern Pacific Railway, and, travelling all night, we found ourselves, on awakening in the morning, on the plains of the Red River Valley where a beautiful panorama was unfolded to our view. On every side we were surrounded by slight undulating plains which extended as far as the eye could reach. These plains are not like some in other parts of the world, which consisting of a light, sandy soil, lose their rich green appearance under the influence of the sun's rays; but, the soil being very deep and rich, the grass does not lose its freshness during the whole summer, and consequently attains a prodigious height; three tons of hay to the acre, being no uncommon yield.

While I was reflecting on the bright future of this country, we came in sight of Red River, of which I will here give a brief description as we are about to travel for some days along the banks.

Red River rises near the source of the Mississippi. At first it flows in a south-westerly direction, then turns to the north and keeps that direction until it empties its waters into Lake Winnipeg. In proportion as this river recedes from its source, the region that it waters becomes more and more fertile, and the fertility of the soil reaches its maximum in the Province of Manitoba which is traversed by this stream. Along its course this river receives the waters of a great number of streams, the most

2'

important of which, are : on the right shore, Red Lake
River, the Roseau, and the Rat River ; on the left shore,
the Sheyenne, the Pembina, and the Assinaboine. The
course of Red River is about 500 miles in length, and, in
summer time, several steamboats plough its waters between Moorhead and Dufferin.

About ten o'clock, the same morning, we reached Fargo,
then a small village, but now a flourishing town on Red
River. This station, which is about 1300 miles distant
from Toronto, was the farthest point on our journey that
we could reach by rail. We had, therefore, to depend
upon our horses and waggons to complete our journey to
Dufferin, Manitoba, where the three divisions which had
been organised at the Stone Fort were waiting for us.
Dufferin is 150 miles distant from Fargo, and the shortest road connecting these two places lies along the left
shore of Red River.

On our arrival in Fargo the first thing we did was to
take out the horses and turn them loose on the prairie.
Next, we unloaded our goods, the most of which were to
be conveyed down the river by the steamboat as far as
Dufferin, and the remainder in our waggons. When the
unloading was finished, the stores covered a good many
acres of ground : a sight which greatly pleased the inhabitants of Fargo, who, thinking that we would be detained
there several days, were figuring, like true Yankees, how
many dollars they would make by our long stay. But
they little knew what Canadians could do, when properly
directed. The Commissioner ordered that fatigue parties

should be organised, each of them working four hours without intermission, and resting the next four. By these means, the work was done with such alacrity, that on the evening of the 14th, two days after our arrival at Fargo, the three divisions were *en route* for Dufferin.

We proceeded about six miles when we pitched our tents and prepared our evening meal for the first time in the open prairie. With the exception of a few who took part in the Red River expedition of 1870, we knew nothing about prairie life, so the greatest tumult I ever witnessed reigned for a time among us. Constables were shouting for night sentries, cooks were calling for wood and water, while at the same time, just by them, was flowing the river, whose banks were covered with fuel. Everything in fact was in confusion that evening. After many ups and downs order was at last restored. In the centre of our encampment was an enclosure made with a large cable and stakes, where the horses were confined for the night. An outer enclosure was made by the waggons, a passage being left at each corner, where the sentries were stationed. This enclosure was intended to answer two purposes : first, to keep the horses from running away, if from fright or any other cause, they should break through the inner one ; and second, to be used as a kind of breastwork if we should be attacked by the Indians. These precautions being taken, the bugle called us to our evening meal.

A repast on the prairies of the North-West had for us, at least, the charm of novelty. Let the reader represent to himself men seated in groups around several fires, each having a large cup of tea and a tin plate holding a slice of bacon and two or three biscuits, and he will have an idea of the food on which we had to live during our journey. Such a plain and frugal meal aroused murmurs among the more fastidious. Some were complaining of the quality of the food, and some of the scant quantity. "Does the government take us for slaves by giving us such victuals ?" says one of the former. "They must think we are babies by giving us such scanty meals," says one of the latter.

The grumbling was increasing, when a constable, an old veteran of the Six Hundred Light Brigade, interposed and asked what was the matter. One of them said he would die before he would try to live on bacon. "Oh no," said he, "you spoiled child of your mother, before many days are over, a slice of bacon will be as welcome as a piece of chicken." Then turning to those who were complaining of the small quantity of food, he said : "If you are dissatisfied now, what will your feelings be when you have nothing to eat." Later on we were to realise the truth of these last words ; but more of this hereafter. With the above the disagreeable question ended, and all, except the sentries, retired to rest.

During the summer season the climate in the North-West is very different from that of Ontario. While in Ontario the summer nights are as warm as in the tropical zone, in the North-West Territories the nights are cold, the atmosphere is clear and bracing, and the sky is bril-

liant as a diamond. From this you will perceive that,
each of us being provided with two blankets, our first
camping night was very agreeable. This was plainly de-
monstrated in the morning; for, when the trumpeter
sounded the reveillé, nearly every one was soundly sleeping, and some were even then unwilling to rise.

After breakfast the camp broke up and the three divisions resumed their march. Men and horses were in good
spirits, the road was in good condition, and everything
promised a successful journey. From time to time the
monotony of the journey was broken by the sight of deserted shanties, which had been inhabited by hunters and
trappers, when buffaloes were roaming in that region.

A great deal has been said and written about these adventurous characters, forerunners of civilisation on the
American continent. Some of them, if we are to believe
certain writers, formerly belonged to the European no-
bility, and, becoming tired of civilisation, came out to
pass the remainder of their lives among the Indians. This
opinion, doubtless, originated in the imagination of the
above writers. Yet I admit that there has been, and
there are still men who, though used to the comforts of
refined life, will, for novelty sake, go and live for a few
years in a wild country; but when they go back to their
former life they will appreciate the more its superiority
and advantages. In reality, most of the hunters and
trappers were men of small means in their native countries. But hearing of the natural riches of the new continent, they came over to seek their fortunes. Most of

them failed in their objects, and unable, for want of pecuniary means, to get back to their native lands, they married Indian women and settled down to the wild life of the hunter. From these alliances originated the greater part of the half-breed population which spreads over the semi-wild regions of America.

But to go back to our journey. That day we travelled thirty miles. Rather a long march for horses that had just ended a long journey by railway, and after leaving Fargo, living on grass too tender yet to be substantial. Furthermore, most of them were not broken to harness. The same speed was kept up the two following days; the result being that the horses failed rapidly in flesh and in strength. On the morning of the 18th we found many of them disabled, and two of them went down to rise no more. The reasons the Commissioner had for ordering such marches are still a mystery to me; for, if water was sometimes scarce along the road, the river being almost always in view, could easily be reached across the prairie.

The capacity of Col. French, as commander of the expedition, was already being questioned among the men. We began to discuss what would become of us if, when once on the vast prairies, several hundred miles from human help, he would attempt to make marches such as we were then experiencing.

The disabled horses being unable to go as fast as the rest, were left to follow behind in charge of a small party of men, and it fell to my lot to be one of them. As for the main body, they went on as fast as before, and reached

Dufferin on the evening of the 19th of June. The next day we also arrived with our sick horses. There we remained long enough to have a good rest; but the particulars of our stay will be related in our next chapter.

CHAPTER III.

DUFFERIN, which is situated near the national boundary, at the junction of the Pembina and Red rivers, was of small account in 1874; a Government warehouse, a Hudson Bay Company store, two whiskey saloons, and a few log shanties, inhabited by half breeds, being the only buildings then in existence. As Dufferin could be reached by steamboat, and being at the same time the nearest and most convenient way of approach to the south-western part of Manitoba, it was chosen in 1876 as the principal landing place for intending settlers in the North-West. This selection contributed to a great extent, to make of Dufferin a flourishing little town.

The night of our arrival there was dark and sultry, and, during the day, the sky had been overcast with clouds, infallible indications of an approaching storm. About eight o'clock, we led the horses into the inner inclosure already described, and made them fast to the cable. Then the guard was set, one half watching the horses, the other half guarding the approaches of the camp, and the rest of us retired to rest, feeling greatly in need of it, after the forced march that we had just experienced.

The night, as I have said, was extremely dark, and about ten o'clock, daylight having entirely disappeared, we were rapt in utter gloom, with nothing to disturb the stillness, save the usual calls of the sentries. But very soon, distant but distinct peals of thunder were heard. In this country, storms rage with a fierceness and fury seldom witnessed in other countries, and even the native animals are filled with fear at their approach. Our horses soon gave signs of uneasiness, and the fright increased as the peals of thunder became louder and louder. The sentries, efforts to calm them were vain; the poor brutes no longer recognised the human voice. A prey to intense fear which inspired them with unusual strength, they broke their halters, trampled the sentries under foot, overturned two or three waggons, and madly rushed, with the speed of wind, over the open prairie. The bugle sounded the alarm; and in a few minutes, we were in rank, expecting to have to fight the Sioux Indians who were said to be in the neighbourhood. But we soon discovered that the alarm was occasioned by a stampede among the horses, and that we were required to search for, and recovered the terrified animals, and not to fight the Indians. At that moment we were spectators of a scene which will be never forgotten by those who witnessed it. A dazzling and continuous glare of lightning, which seemed like one sheet of fire above our heads; crashes of thunder which appeared to shake the earth to its very centre, and a hurricane which, in spite of our utmost efforts, blew down our tents, formed an imposing sight, capable of frightening men less resolute than ourselves.

A few horses remained in the corral, whether because they were less strong than the others, or more firmly tied I cannot say, and with these, a few of us set out in search of the others. Our attepmts that night were fruitless; but after three days of hard riding, and search, we succeeded in recovering all but one, which, in his mad fright, had rushed into the Pembina river, and was drowned.

After removing our camp to a more convenient place the final organisation of the six divisions into one force was begun.

The six divisions were designated by the first six letters of the alphabet : A B and C representing the divisions organized at the Stone Fort; D E F representing those organised at Toronto. During their stay at the Stone Fort, the divisions A B and C lost about thirty men, who with the exception of a few who applied for their discharge, were dismissed for bad conduct, or for being unable to perform their duties. This, and the expectation that some desertions would occur during our journey, and during our stay at Dufferin, explains why, on leaving Toronto, our company contained fifty-one extra men.

Transferring from our divisions to those from Winnipeg, until their numbers were completed, we still had twenty men more than we required; but being near the international boundary, frequent desertions occurred, and we were soon reduced to no more than fifty men in each division.

As travelling in the North-West was at that time, and is yet, very difficult on account of the bad state of the roads, the Commissioner was invested with full powers to let tenders for the transfer of our supplies to any part of the territory where they might be needed. But Colonel French, under the circumstances, showed great want of ability as Commander-in-Chief. For, instead of taking into consideration the miserable state to which the horses were reduced by the journey from Fargo to Dufferin, he directed that every division should take with it a dozen waggons, each carrying a ton of freight, and all drawn by the horses alloted to that division. A large portion of our supplies was to be taken in this manner, and the remainder was to be taken by a few more waggons, and 114 carts drawn by oxen. The carts, to each of which was to be attached a single ox, were to be driven by half-breeds hired for that purpose.

From my position in Division B, to which I had been transferred, I heard one morning a great uproar in Division A camping near by. Wishing to know the cause, I went out, and meeting a comrade of that division, who was splitting his sides with laughter, I enquired what it was all about. He replied : "It is a long story. You have brought us from Toronto an original character. Since his transfer to our division, he does nothing but preach temperance, and remind us of the noble duties which we are called upon to perform. Some compare him to Don Quixotte, but others of more reflective minds, say that before judging him we must see him at work. I was on

duty last night when, about midnight, I suddenly saw
issuing from our tent an individual clothed in white, who,
after glancing rapidly on every side, made a dash through
the sentry line, and out on the prairie. I thought to myself, here is one who has soon forgotten the regulations
he will doubtlessly return, and I shall know who he is.
Without suspecting him of having any complicity with
the Indians, I watched him closely. Returning at last I
arrested him at the entrance to the Camp, with the usual
challenge, 'Who comes there?' The fellow appeared
disconcerted; but finding himself threatened with being
marched off to the guardhouse, he declared himself a
member of the Mounted Police. 'Give me the password,'
said I; but this he was unable to do. I was going to call
the guard, when seeing him shivering with cold, I took
pity on him and allowed him to pass, laughing to myself
at the thought of the merriment which would be produced
by relating the story of his spending the night on the
prairie in his night-shirt. Everything turned out as I
expected, and my story was received with the uproarious
laughter that brought you from your quarters. 'Zounds!'
said one, 'I understand now why this fellow wears a night-
shirt; it is to scare the Indians. See how cunning he is.
If the Indians attack us, and are repelled, very well; but
if it happens to the contrary, I would not give much for
our scalps,—but he, on account of his night-shirt, will be
looked upon as the Great Manitou of the whites and will
remain unmolested.' Look over there! Don Quixotte
is on sentry; no better selection could be made after the

massacre perpetrated at St. Ives by the Sioux a few days ago."

Looking in the direction indicated, I saw a sub-constable of military appearance, walking along the sentry line, watching the surroundings of the camp, and glancing once in a while with a wistful look at his carbine and revolver, which indicated a longing to use them. "What!" said I to myself, "can this man be the Apostle of Temperance"? It was, indeed, but what a metamorphosis since our first meeting! The clergyman was no more, and there remained but the soldier. I was going to congratulate him on his martial appearance, when an Inspector intervened. "Sub-constable L.," said he, "what are you thinking about to mount guard with your carbine full cocked?" "Sir" replied our templar, "In circumstances such as these, in which we find ourselves at present in danger of being attacked at any time by Indians, one cannot be too well prepared to fire." The Inspector had to treat our warrior with arrest before he could make him understand the danger of carrying fire-arms full cocked.

The same day, in the afternoon, the news was spread that the Sioux were marching towards our camp, with hostile intentions. The Commissioner ordered us to be ready at once to meet the enemy. The horses, which were grazing about a mile from the camp, were brought in immediately, and before long Division A stood in two ranks ready to march. Colonel French praised the men of this division for their soldier-like appearance and their

speed in getting ready to take the field. Very soon, the
other divisions were ready, and the word of command
was given. Division A moved first, followed closely by
the others in alphabetical order. This was in July.
The horses had regained their wonted strength, and
showed anxiety for action. As we were going along,
some field manœuvres were attempted ; not very successfully, I must say, but how could it be otherwise,—men
and horses cannot be well trained in three months' time
for military service. Notwithstanding some defects, we
did very well, and at all events we were soldiers at heart,
which is the best proficiency for men in warfare. We expected to have to fight, and were ready to do it to the
best of our ability. The following dialogue will give an
idea of the state of our feelings at that moment. "Did
you take any part in the Franco-German war ?" said a
constable at my side. "No, indeed," I replied, "this is my
first experience in warfare." "So it is with me," said he,
'I long to see if the Indians have as good hands and
eyes for warfare as the Canadians. It is going to be hot
work, I fancy, for I hear the Sioux are well equipped
and are good horsemen."

Being by this time two or three miles from the camp,
in the open prairie, the command to deploy was given. I
expected, at any moment, to see Indians, as I had read of
them in the novels, springing from the grass with their
war-whoops, and charging us with their tomahawks ; but
I was disappointed in my expectations. We hunted the
plain for miles around until sun-set, without the appear-

ance of Indians, when, to the great dissatisfaction of all, the order was given to return to camp.

This turning out was only a sham; the Commissioner, thinking that there were still a few cowards in our ranks, and wishing to get rid of them, spread the news himself that the Sioux were in the neighbourhood, and in a state of hostility. But he was agreeably disappointed in finding that there was not a coward among us, and that every man, while knowing that he could safely get away, remained at his post.

CHAPTER IV.

IN the afternoon of the 8th of July, the organisation being completed, the Mounted Police started from Dufferin directing their march towards Roche Percée, which lies 270 miles west, where sub-Inspector S. from Fort Ellice was to meet us with fresh horses. Division A with thirteen waggons marched first, closely followed by the other divisions in regular order. In front, and on the flanks of the column rode a guard of twenty men charged to open the march, and to prevent surprises. Behind the last division, came the half-breeds with their Red River carts, and, at some distance behind them, a herd of cattle, driven by the rear guard. This was the first column of troops that ever marched on the plains of the North-West. A splendid sight; but destined to last but a short time.

We camped that night about three miles from Dufferin. A short journey indeed, but nevertheless long enough for the horses which, as I said before, were not well used to harness, and had to draw overloaded waggons. The conduct of Colonel French, in regard to the final organization of the company at Dufferin, was far from being approved by his subordinate officers ; an outburst of revolt was then expected, and the expected revolt occurred the next morning before setting out.

The Commissioner had ordered the Inspectors to provide every morning a necessary number of horses for the waggons. Inspector Richer of F Division, being well aware that, if these commands were obeyed, the men would soon be on foot, was not in a hurry to produce the number of horses required, and an altercation ensued between him and Colonel French. But notwithstanding his many faults, the Commissioner was a well disciplined and experienced officer, and, knowing well that if this disobedience remained unpunished he would soon have to face revolts of a more serious character, he put Inspector Richer under arrest. This we did not expect he would dare to do, as this officer was known to be well backed by men of high standing in the Government. In spite of his arrest, Inspector Richer left at once for Dufferin, threatening, as soon as he should arrive in Ottawa, to acquaint the government with the real state of the Mounted Police.

On the morning of the third day, we came in view of the vast plain which is bounded on the west by what is called the Pembina Mountains,—in reality a range of hills, not more than forty to fifty feet above the level of the plains. As no wood could be found in the neighbourhood, the Commissioner ordered us to take with us a sufficient

3

quantity of wood to last two days. Proceeding on our
way, we at times came across large quantities of buffalo
bones, which gave us an idea of the immense slaughter of
these animals that must have occurred there in fŏrmer
years, and was then being carried on in the neighbourhood of the Rocky Mountains, to which locality they had
been driven. The plain, which we were crossing, although
very fertile, was at that time almost entirely without
water, the meadow lands, usually covered with a few
inches, being dried up. Happily, at night, we came to
one of these meadows, the centre of which contained
enough water, such as it was, to keep the men from suffering with thirst, but the horses and cattle had to do
without. I say such as it was,—for after being taken
from the hole dug to receive it, and strained, it was still
as black as ink.

The next morning at eleven o'clock, we reached Pembina Mountain Depot, where we found water in abundance. The last two days had been hard enough on the
men, but still more so on the horses and cattle which had
suffered greatly from want of water. We naturally expected to rest there a day or two ; but the Commissioner
decided that the march should be resumed immediately
after dinner. Probably he compared himself to conquerors
like Alexander and Cæsar, and wanted to leave in the
shade the marches of these illustrious men.

We reached the banks of the Pembina river, at this
place only about fifteen feet wide. A bridge had been
thrown across it some years before, but it was now in

such a wretched condition, we thought it unsafe to cross before the bridge was re-constructed. A party of men was therefore detailed to do this work, and also, to improve the road up the opposite bank. This done, we crossed the river in the evening, and in ascending the bank, we found the oxen of great service. Taking a yoke of them in front of the horses, we would hook the chain in the end of the waggon-tongue, and with this double team, take the loads up the steep bank very easily. At sunset, we camped about five miles further on. During the whole night, our half-breeds kept coming into camp with their carts. This shows the difficulty they encountered in climbing the river bank.

In my travels in the North-West, I noticed that even the smallest streams have very high banks, which seems to me to prove that they once carried a much greater quantity of water than they now do. In rivers, like the Pembina, which do not rise among mountains, covered with eternal snows, these large bodies of water could only be produced by very abundant rains. But as such abundant rains are only to be met with in very warm countries, we would naturally conclude that there has been a time when the climate in that section was much more mild than it is now.

Hitherto we had passed through plains that were very fertile ; but we were now in a region that was quite the contrary, and the oats, which we had brought with us, being now consumed, our horses were left in a sad plight for want of sufficient provender. Besides this, many of

the horses were already tired out, and we therefore expected we would rest at least two or three days, to give
them time to recruit. But Colonel French not only gave
orders that we should march at once, but inflicted upon
us an indignity which took from us all the pride we felt
in being members of the Mounted Police. The reason
why the half-breeds were so late in reaching camp every
night, was that each of them had to drive four carts ; and
in order to remedy this, the Commissioner gave orders
that each division should provide a certain number of
men to assist them. It is useless to mention how we
greeted such an order, and I believe had we not been a
long distance from any settlement, the Colonel would
have had to make the expedition alone. What military
commander, who respects his men and wants to be re-
spected by them, would have thought (I do not say dare)
to have placed them on the same footing as those who
worked for mercenary motives. The members of the
Mounted Police had sworn to keep the British flag un-
stained ; while the half-breeds had only engaged to work
for so many dollars a month. No comparison could, therefore, be made between us ; and it was more than discour-
aging, on the morning of the 15th to see some of our men,
in their uniforms, driving oxen with sticks. And yet,
notwithstanding my disgust, I could not help being somewhat interested and amused when, the next morning, it
fell to my lot to drive a train of these carts. Being a
new hand at the work, the foreman of the half-breeds very
kindly harnessed my oxen, and arranged them in order

for starting, the strongest ox in front, the next strongest tied to the back of the first one's cart, and the weakest one behind and that tied to the second cart. On starting we received three biscuits each, on which to make our noonday meal, it being expected that we could not keep up with the main column, and be able to take our dinner with them.

I would here like to describe the noise made by the carts, but words fail me. It must be heard to be understood. A den of wild beasts cannot be compared with it in hideousness. Combine all the discordant sounds ever heard in Ontario and they cannot produce anything so horrid as a train of Red River carts. At each turn of the wheel, they run up and down all the notes of the scale in one continuous screech, without sounding distinctly any note or giving one harmonious sound. And this unearthly discord is so loud, that a train of carts, coming towards you can be heard long before they are seen. We travelled a long distance that day, and the waggons going faster than our carts, they were entirely out of our sight at nightfall; our oxen being tired out, we were obliged to camp out of sight of the camp fires of our comrades; and not only this, but our provisions and blankets being on the waggons of the main column, we had to lie down supperless on the bare ground, and in that manner pass the night.

In such circumstances as these, one appreciates the society of a man who preserves, through every vicissitude of life, his habitual philosophy. Among us was one

whose indifference to hardship contrasted greatly with
the dissatisfaction and grumbling of his companions.
" My friends," said he at last, " you do nothing but grum-
ble, now against the Government, and then the Commissioner, but you should remember we were prepared
for this before leaving Toronto, If my memory serves
me rightly, the Colonel told us then that we might at
times, be without food for two or three days at a time, and
have to camp on the open prairie with nothing but the
canopy of heaven for covering; and he added that if any
of us were not willing to face those hardships and
probably many others, we might return to our homes.
Of what do you complain then ? "   " We complain," said
one more touchy than the rest, " of having to drive ox-
carts."   " Do you think then," replied our modern
Diogenes, " that it is not preferable to perform the duties
of an ox-driver than to sleep in the open air, and be
several days without food ?   If you do, I am not of your
opinion."   " It seems to me," said I, " that you see only
one side of the question ; you forget that if the Sioux
were in the neighbourhood, they could easily get the
better of us, and take possession of the oxen and carts
that are scattered along the road for several miles."   " I
don't forget that either," said he, " but on hearing the
Commissioner speak about the privations to be endured
should we not have expected dangers as well, and all the
more inevitable too since we were to travel through
Indian Territories !   Let us hope that we shall not find
ourselves in more critical circumstances than at present."

These judicious observations had the effect of reconciling us to our situation, if one can judge from the sonorous snores which followed.   For my part, the remembrance of our proximity to the Sioux Territory, and especially the late massacres perpetrated by those savages, prevented me from sleeping.   But at that season of the year a night quickly passes, and when morning dawned, seeing that no one wished to rise, I harnessed my oxen and set out again, hoping to overtake the main column before they broke up camp.   But my designs were frustrated, and I found the camp deserted, the want of water having obliged them to set out early.   Increasing the pace of my oxen I continued to advance, and then began in reality the hardships of privation.   I was all day consumed by a thirst that all the ravines which I crossed could not quench.   When night came two of my oxen were tired out.   What was I to do?   Beat them unmercifully as the half-breeds did till they would fall?   I had not sunk to such a degree of cruelty.   I chose the wisest course, set them at liberty, and with the third proceeded as fast as possible on my journey.   About eleven o'clock the sight of deserted waggons proved that I was not far from the camp, though I could not as yet see their fires.   Very soon, however, I was arrested by the usual challenge: " Who comes there?"   " A famished man," I replied, and the sentry allowed me to pass without further explanation.

They had located their camp in a valley, on the banks of a small brook.   The men were lying around the camp fires, being too fatigued to set up the tents. It mattered very little to me where I slept, the main point being to get something to eat from the kettles which remained near the half-extinguished fires. My search was at first fruitless, and I visited no less than five divisions before finding provisions at the sixth. Stealing my way over the sleeping men, I found a large kettle of cooked meat, a box of bread, and a kettle of tea. Seated on the ground, with the meat between my knees, the bread on one side, and the tea on the other, I made a meal that only a hearty man, having been two days without food, could dispose of. In fact, it was nearly daylight when I had fully satisfied my appetite, and, making my way to my own division, I climbed into a waggon and was soon fast asleep.

A little after sunrise the column resumed its march, notwithstanding the fact that a large number of carts were still miles behind. Having done more than my share of ox-driving I was allowed to follow my waggon on foot, I say on foot, and a large number of the men were doing the same; for the Commissioner, on account of the wretched condition of the horses, had ordered that one of the two men accompanying every waggon should walk while the other drove; and, to be certain that his orders were carried out, the Colonel would ride, once in a while, from front to rear and back. That morning, as he was making his first round, he noticed a waggon with only the driver in sight. He at once rode up and asked the driver who was his comrade and where he was. " Constable S., sir," said the driver, "and he is lying inside of the wag-gon." "What!" said the Colonel, " a constable the first to break my commands! Come down at once," said he to Constable S., "or I will put you under arrest," " I don't care what you do," answered Constable S., " I joined a *mounted* police and not a *foot* one, and, as I don't feel very well to-day, I must ride on something, a horse or a wag-gon, I don't care which." Upon this rebuke, the Commis-sioner rode away ; a proof that he was fast losing his in-fluence over the men.

In the evening of the following day we reached the Souris river, a tributary of the Assiniboine. Since Duf-ferin, it was the most favourable place to camp that we had met. Wood, water and grass were abundant, and the Commissioner decided we should remain there two days. Two reasons rendered this halt necessary : first, many of the horses were so exhausted that they were unable to proceed; and second, because the carts were still far be-hind, and a great number of them had to be repaired. Though the next day was Sunday the men were kept busy, washing themselves and their clothes, and looking after the horses.

On Monday, the usual monotony of the camp life was dis-turbed by the report that the Sioux were following us, though without daring to attack. The originator of this re-port was Sub-constable P., who had been in charge of a number of sick horses. As he could not travel so fast as the main body he found himself the day previous to our arrival at the Souris river, some thirty miles behind, and during the day one of the sick horses fell to rise no more. What could he do ? Certainly his orders were to remain there until some one was sent to his rescue. But then, he was alone, unprotected and without provisions. So he concluded the best thing to do was to shoot the poor dying brute, and proceed on his journey. Being well aware that if he told what he had done the Commissioner would not only fine him, but make him pay about two hundred dollars for the horse, he declared with great earnestness that he had been attacked by five Sioux, and that, making a vigorous resistance, he won the day, losing nothing but one horse which was killed in the fight. Every one was convinced that his story was a fabrication but nobody could prove it.

On Tuesday the whole column resumed the march, the last of the carts having arrived in camp sometime during the previous night ; and finally on Friday, the 24th of July, we arrived at Roche Percée. But what a change since our departure from Dufferin ! We had set out full of hope, mounted on excellent horses, accompanied by waggons carrying our supplies, and followed by carts laden with the same, but our hopes were doomed to bitter disappointment. No romantic incidents occurred; no encounter with the Indians and the whiskey-traders, and on our arrival at Roche Percée the column resembled a routed army corps. For a distance of several miles the road was strewed with broken carts, and horses and oxen overcome with hunger and fatigue. This was the natural result of the Commissioner's blunder before leaving Dufferin, in ordering us to carry our supplies. During the whole of Saturday, horses and oxen which had been unable to keep up to the column, continued to arrive in a deplorable condition. Was it in this manner that the Canadian Government had intended the Mounted Police to be managed and directed? Certainly not! Could Colonel French have done better than he did? Certainly yes! for although it is always a difficult matter to judge fairly the conduct of a commander-in-chief, I think I can safely say, and hope to prove it farther on, that other officers of our force could have done better than he.

CHAPTER V.

Report that the Mounted Police had been Massacred by the Sioux—Roche Percée—Church Services—The Division of Our Forces.

SATURDAY evening, following our arrival at Roche Percée, we were overtaken by Dr. N. and Constable C. who had left Dufferin a week after we did. They brought the news that, when they left, a report was in circulation through the American newspapers, that the Mounted Police had been exterminated by the Sioux. This report originated from deserters, who had left us at Dufferin, and, having gone across the lines, had given as reasons for deserting, that they were badly treated, and that they did not wish to lose their scalps in the projected expedition against the whiskey traders. One can easily conceive that the Americans, who are continually at war with their own Indians, would have been glad to see our expedition miscarry. Therefore, the reports of the deserters were grossly exaggerated by the American papers which, having summed up the various difficulties that we would have to overcome, some of them concluded that we would be unsuccesful, and others that we were already exterminated. The Canadian public, considering the suspicious origin of these stories, put very little faith in them. But, later on, great uneasiness was felt through the country, when it became known that the road taken by the Mounted Police was through Sioux territory, and along the international boundary. Prayers for us were said in some Canadian churches, and some leading minds went so far as to advocate the organization of a corps of volunteers to avenge us. But this project was never carried into effect ; for, as soon as we arrived at Roche Percée, the Commissioner sent despatches to the Government, announcing our arrival there in good health and spirits.

The column was encamped on the banks of the Souris River, in a circular valley surrounded on almost every side by a range of hills some thirty to forty feet in height. Wood, water and grass were abundant, and coal also could be gathered on the right bank of the river. The quality of this coal was tested by our blacksmiths who used it during our stay there. Although this coal, on account of its friability, is not likely to be exported any great distance, it will nevertheless be a great boon for the settlers in that region, where wood will soon be scarce.

On our right, and about half a mile from the camp, stood Roche Percée, a pierced rock, as its name indicates. Seen from a distance, one would take it for a statue, whose arms rested on two adjacent supports. An isolated rock, in the midst of a plain, will naturally attract the attention of a traveller : and in company with some of my comrades, I went to visit this one, which is covered with hieroglyphic characters, indecipherable for us, but

doubtlessly representing memorable events that once took
place in that country.

The third day after our arrival being a Sunday, and,
as everybody is aware, the Sabbath day being consecrated
in the British Dominions to rest and prayer, we were
that morning ordered to get ready for Church parade.
This was the first divine service held since our departure
from Dufferin. As the Mounted Police was composed of
men belonging to different denominations, and there being
no chaplain attached to the corps, I was wondering who
would act in their stead. But I soon heard that, under
such circumstances, it was the duty of officers to act in
the place of ministers of the gospel. At ten o'clock a.m.
as the six divisions stood ready for orders, Colonel
French, who was an Episcopalian, called for the men that
belonged to his denomination, and Roman Catholics,
Methodists, and Presbyterians were called for, in like
manner by officers of their respective creeds. Some denominations held their meetings on the hills, others in
the valley. And it was a grand sight to see 300 men
standing in the wilderness, several hundred miles from
civilization, giving thanks, in different manners, and offering prayer to their Creator. Although several thousand miles separated us from our friends in the other provinces, our thoughts and hearts were with theirs, and
their prayers and ours were of like nature, and had in
view our preservation and the success of the expedition.

The plan of the campaign furnished to the Commissioner by the Government at the time of our organization

was the following :—We were to proceed from Dufferin as far as the junction of the rivers Bow and Belly, where the whiskey traders were said to congregate, destroy their forts and leave in that section a sufficient number of men to put an end to the massacres and the whiskey traffic. But, about the time of our departure from Dufferin, Colonel French received new instructions from the Government, slightly altering the above plan. After demolishing the whiskey traders' forts, half of the column was to proceed to Edmonton, and the other half to retrace their steps homeward.

The junction of the above rivers, is about 450 miles distant from Roche Percée ; and between these two localities lay vast plains almost destitute of water, wood and grass. At that time, there was no cart road connecting Roche Percée and the junction of these rivers, and the latter place was almost unknown to even the fur-traders. Edmonton is about 200 miles further on from the junction ; and part of this distance had also to be travelled without any road to guide us. Adding the two preceding distances, we find that half of our corps had still to travel about 650 miles before reaching its destination, and the other half 450 miles, and then return homeward.

The three divisions intended for Edmonton, were expected to take with them all the supplies we had brought from Dufferin. Now, if we take into consideration the critical state to which the horses and oxen had been reduced by the journey from Dufferin to Roche Percée, a distance of only 270 miles, any one could see that it would

be impossible for us to take our supplies *via* the junction.
But then how were the three divisions intended for Edmonton to be without supplies? Colonel French was thus
placed in a very awkward predicament. He could now
see plainly the folly of his management in the outset;
neither horses nor men could be hired at Roche Percée,
and even the fresh horses that we expected from Fort
Ellice were not forthcoming; Sub-inspector S., who was to
have brought them, came himself and reported that he
had been obliged to send the horses he had to Winnipeg
for fresh supplies. Under these circumstances, the Commissioner adopted the most unreasonable and incredible
plan that ever originated in any man's brain—placing in
the hands of Inspector Jarvis a dozen good men of his
own division, with instructions to proceed to Edmonton,
via Fort Ellice, with twenty-four waggons, fifty-four carts,
fifty-five of the weakest horses, a large number of oxen,
and a herd of cows and calves. A dozen half-breeds were
also given him to assist in driving the carts; and besides
the above, he was instructed to take as far as Fort Ellice,
five or six sick men and two or three waggons. As for
myself, although a member of B Division, for some reason
never made known to me, I was transferred to Inspector
Jarvis' command.

Having only sick horses, or horses reduced to mere
skeletons, and considering we were going *via* Fort Ellice,
and thus would have to travel at least nine hundred miles
before reaching our destination, was it reasonable on the
part of Colonel French, to expect us to reach Edmonton

before the coming winter ? For my part, I do not think
he expected for a moment that we would be able to go
any farther than Fort Ellice, a distance of 130 miles from
Roche Percée. But if he did, he thereby tacitly acknowledged that Inspector Jarvis was better able than he to
direct the expedition. For travelling 900 miles with
sick horses and heavy waggons was a very different
thing from travelling 270 miles with horses that were at
least in good condition at the outset. But, notwithstanding all these disadvantages, we shall see, later on, how
successfully Inspector Jarvis conducted his party to their
destination.

CHAPTER VI.

Departure of the Main Column from Roche Percée—The Templar's Castles in the Air Vanish—Departure of Our Party for Fort Ellice—A Change for the Better—The Glorious Death of a Sioux Brave—A Horrible Dream.

ON THE 29th of July, the main column resumed its march under the command of the Commissioner, and on reaching the plains, they left the international boundary line, taking a north-western course towards the junction. We will now leave, for a while, these men, who were destined to encounter hardships unsurpassed in the history of man, and we will return to the little party, under the command of inspector Jarvis, still encamped at Roche Percée.

I learned from some of the men that the Apostle of Temperance was one of our party; and, wishing to know what he now thought of the great mission of the Mounted Police, I was very anxious to see him. But I had some difficulty in finding him; nobody could tell me where he was. Giving up the search, I was returning to my quarters, when seated on a hill that faces Roche Percée, I beheld a member of the Mounted Police who appeared very much absorbed in thought. I went up to him, and, sure enough, he was the man I sought. "Well

my friend," said I, " I am very glad to hear that you are
going with us to Edmonton." But, seeing that he took
no notice of my remark, I shook him, shouting at this
time : " Ha ! father of the braves, are you asleep." He
lifted up his eyes, giving me a reproachful look, as much
as to say : " how dare you disturb my reveries," and sorry
to have gone so far, I was about to apologize for the
liberty I had taken, when he now seemed to realize that
no offence was intended, for his face assumed a mild
appearance, and, as an answer to my enquiry, said :
" would to God I had never seen this day." " Why, what
is the matter with you ? " said I. " Why do you ask me
that question ? " said he, " don't you know as well as I ?
Have you not also been detached from the main column,
where glory awaited us, to go, not to Edmonton, for we
can never reach there, but to Fort Ellice, which place we
may reach, but never pass, at least this year ! " " But
then," said I, " if we did not go, other men would have to
go in our stead." " All I have to say is this," said he,
" if the corps had been well directed, it would not have
been necessary to send this detatchment to Ellice. All
this is the result of having taken with us our supplies.
Now the evil is without remedy, and if the whiskey
traders are as well organized as they are said to be, the
expedition will surely prove a failure." This said, the
templar resumed his thoughtful appearance, heedless of
my presence. I therefore returned to the camp, reflecting on what a change had come over this man in so short
a time. On our first meeting in the cars, he was full of

hope, and possessed a fine appearance ; but now he was completely discouraged ; his castles in the air had vanished, and his person displayed the utmost neglect." "What is the cause of all this," thought I, and I found the answer in the mismanagement of our commander-in-chief.

The day after the main column left for their destination, we set out for Fort Ellice. Before us was the Souris River which we had to cross. Our horses were too weak to draw the waggons up the bank, but we had four yoke of oxen in pretty fair condition, and, hitching them to the waggons, we were soon safely across. We had to go a day's journey without a road, but we were fortunate in having a half-breed who had come from Fort Ellice, as guide, and resigning ourselves to his direction, we reached the road in safety.

The country that lies between Roche Percée and Fort Ellice is not equal in fertility to the Red River Valley. Wood and grass are not always plentiful, and water is also scarce in summer time. To travel in such a country under these disadvantages and labouring under the unfavourable circumstances in which we were then, required a leader of sound judgment, and great ability. And such a man we had in Inspector Jarvis. He was as fond of short marches as Colonel French was of long ones ; and he was right ; for the proverb, "slow but sure" is always the safest to follow in long marches. Taking advantage of the best camping places to be found, Inspector Jarvis would order a halt, four or five times a day in order to

give the horses and oxen time to feed. And the result of
such a course was soon felt ; the animals began to recover
rapidly, and even most of the sick men were soon able to
resume their duties. I must add that since we were de-
tatched from the main column, we were living together
like a family. No more of this quasi-discipline ; no more
days without food. We performed our duties not only
for our country's sake, but to please our commander.
Every heart was beating for Inspector Jarvis, and if he
had asked us to follow him, even to the North Pole, not
one of us would have refused.

After a week's march, we reached Pipestone Creek
whose banks are high and steep. ˙ The crossing presented
serious difficulties ; but officers and men worked so manfully, that in two hours, waggons and carts were on the
other side.—We were then within two days march of
Fort Ellice.

After travelling a few miles from the creek, I saw, on
the left hand side of the road, something resembling a
tombstone, surrounded by a fence. I enquired of our
guide what it was. "What you see," said he, "is the
grave of a famous Sioux warrior. His grandfather and
his father, for a long time, waged war with the United
States. For some time, they were victorious ; but, at
length, they and their tribe were completely overcome,
and, with the exception of the children who were too
young to take any part in the war, not one of the tribe
was left alive,

"The warrior whose grave you see was then but a child. He resolved to die ; he could not survive the ruin of his family. Suicide was within his reach, but that unnatural feature of civilization is unknown among the Indians. He determined to die fighting, but, as his tender years would not allow him to carry arms, on the ashes of his forefathers, he swore eternal enmity to the American troops, and to fight them as soon as he would be old enough to do so. That time came at last. He summoned to a meeting, the few survivors of his tribe, and, in a valiant speech, recalled to their minds the evils inflicted on their forefathers and their glorious resistance. 'For my part,' said he at the conclusion of his harangue, 'I am resolved to die, but to die in avenging our tribe and my family.' This patriotic address received unanimous approval. The hearers resolved to share the fortunes of the speaker and elected him chief. And they had not long to wait before meeting a company of American soldiers whom they attacked with great impetuosity. Their unforeseen attack disconcerted the soldiers at first, but seeing very soon the small number they had to deal with, they manfully stood their ground, and their discipline soon gave them the advantage. At last, every Indian succumbed but the chief, who stood at the entrance of a forest, with his back to a tree, fighting with that energy that only despair can give. A circle of steel is gradually surrounding him ; he sees now that he is going to be taken prisoner, and this is what he dreads,—not death. Flight is still possible, and quickly gathering the arrows of the dead warriors lying around him, he retreated into the forest, resolved on prolonging the unequal contest. He let fly his arrows, which never missed their mark, but at last, he was driven out of the wood, and had no other refuge than the bare plain. The soldiers were reduced to two, but these pursued, resolving to avenge the death of their comrades. After a pursuit of two days, the Indian hides himself in a small thicket ; with his bow bent, he is ready to let fly the two arrows which will give him the victory. But the stratagem is guessed by the two soldiers who have, by this time, learned to be careful—crawling through the grass, one of them got within range, and discharged his rifle. The ball pierced the breast of the savage who, brandishing his tomahawk, bounded toward the enemy. But the wound proved to be mortal, and before reaching his enemy, he fell, to rise no more. So much courage disarmed the rage of the soldiers. They lavished their utmost care upon the Sioux brave, but all in vain, his spirit had already taken its flight, to join his forefathers in the happy hunting grounds."

This narrative was related with such earnestness, that I naturally concluded that the tales written by Cooper and other novelists, might not be exaggerated. I therefore longed to meet some Indians that I might induce them to relate their heroic actions. My wish was soon to be gratified, for I learned from our guide that there were several Sioux families in the neighbourhood of Fort Ellice,—refugees from the United States. Several years

before, these Indians had perpetrated massacres in the
State of Minnesota, and in danger of being taken by the
American soldiers, they had retreated to Canadian territory where protection was afforded them, and, they were
assured, would be afforded them, as long as they continued
in peace.

As we were now approaching the neighbourhood of
these Indians, Inspector Jarvis recommended the sentries
to be carefully on their watch, and the others to sleep with
their arms loaded.   After leaving Roche Percée, I did not
sleep in the tents with the other men, preferring to sleep
outside, under a waggon or a tree.   And that night, after
spreading my blankets under a waggon, I laid down,
placing my loaded carabine on my right side, and my revolver on my left.   Pondering for a while on the narrative I had heard from the guide, I, at last, went to sleep,
and began to dream.   I dreamed that we were encamped
where we were in reality ; that I was under a waggon, and
I saw Indians crawling like snakes through the grass and
coming towards the camp.   Taking hold of my carabine,
I tried to rise, but in vain, I could not move.   I then attempted to shout, but could give no utterance.   I was in
great agony, which was increasing as the Indians were getting nearer and nearer.   Already I could see their painted
faces, their naked breasts, and their heads adorned
with hair and quills.   When within fifty yards of the
camp they suddenly made a bound which was followed
by fearful yells that no pen can describe.   Death stared
me in the face.   I collected all my strength to rise, and

this time succeeded so well, that I fell back senseless to the ground, having knocked my head against the axle of the waggon. When my senses returned. I was still lying on my back, the carabine grasped in my right hand, and the revolver in my left. Everything was still with the exception of the horses which were tied to the waggons and eating the grass we had mowed for them the night before. This was only a dream, but of such a horrible nature, I did not care for a recurrence of it.

In the afternoon of the next day, we reached Fort Ellice, seeing here the first human habitation which we had met since we left Dufferin. I shall give a brief description of this place in the following chapter.

CHAPTER VII.

FORT Ellice is a Hudson Bay Company's trading post, situated on the right shore of the Assiniboine River. It is composed of a few wooden buildings inhabited by the Company's employees, and surrounded by a wooden palisade. For many miles around this fort, the land is not very fertile, and, at the time of our arrival there, the grass was very scarce in that immediate neighbourhood. It was therefore deemed necessary to send the horses and cattle about five miles away where the grass was plentiful. Around that fort, stood several wigwams belonging to the tribe above mentioned. But the Indians were so effeminate, one would never have thought that they were of the same nation that had a few years before committed such depredations in the State of Minnesota. During our stay at Fort Ellice they did nothing but encumber our camp, with their squaws and papooses, and devour the remains of our meals.

On the 20th of August, after having enjoyed a week's rest, we resumed our march, leaving some waggons, and a few of the weakest horses at Fort Ellice. We were then

about 750 miles distant from Edmonton. Under the circumstances in which we were, rendered all the more critical
by the approach of winter and the bad state of the road,
one would think it almost impossible for us to reach that
place before winter set in. But the facility with which
we had traversed the distance from Roche Percée to Fort
Ellice, led us to hope that, under the direction of Inspector
Jarvis, every obstacle would be surmounted.

Two hours of march brought us to the River Qu'Appelle, a tributary of the Assiniboine. Here we met with
our former difficulties in crossing rivers and surmounting
them in the same manner. After the crossing was effected,
although it was yet early in the afternoon, the Inspector
decided to advance no further, convinced that a more
favourable place to camp could not be found for several
miles.

After leaving Qu'Appelle, the only important river
which our road would cross, was the South Saskatchewan
from which we were 350 miles distant. On the plains of
the Souris it would have been easy to travel that distance, but one cannot traverse the region situated between
Qu'Appelle and the South Saskatchewan without encountering serious difficulties. In summer time, water is hard
to be found, wood is scarce in consequence of prairie
fires, and grass grows plentifully only on the marshy
grounds.

After leaving Fort Ellice, Inspector Jarvis was our guide,
he having been to Edmonton the previous year. And
his knowing the road, and the most favourable places for

camping, inspired us with entire confidence in him. In traversing this somewhat barren region, we sometimes had to carry with us a sufficient quantity of water to quench our thirst, sometimes wood for our fires, and sometimes even both, always camping were grass was most plentiful.

During our journey the Sioux of Ellice were often the theme of our conversation. "For Sioux," said a sub-constable one day, "they seem to be very cowardly." "The word cowardly is not expressive enough," said the Apostle of Temperance, "if all the Indians resemble them, I tell you frankly that I would not be afraid to meet a score of such braves." As for the half-breeds they were of a different opinion. They declared that their forefathers had suffered a great deal at the hands of the Sioux, and that to judge rightly of their character, it was necessary to see them engaged in a battle.

The most perfect harmony never ceased to prevail in our ranks, officers and men were equal to the situation, and felt mutual dependence upon each other. Often obliged to make forced marches, in order to reach suitable camping places, some of us would be left far behind, our horses giving out, but the men who reached the camping ground first would hasten back with their teams to help the others in.

After a two weeks' march we reached Touchwood Hills, which lay about half-way between Fort Ellice and the South Saskatchewan. On entering the valley of this river, the country began to improve very much ; grass especially became abundant and accordingly we marched more rapidly, looking forward to reaching the banks of the river, which we succeeded in doing in one week. Here we camped by the side of a band of Cree Indians who were going to hunt buffaloes. A ferry was at our disposal to cross this river, but it being Saturday evening, we had to wait till Monday before ferrying our horses, waggons, and carts across. This delay was very annoying to Inspector Jarvis, for it was then September, and during this month a snow storm invariably arises in those regions, which sometimes lasts for a week. This was what we dreaded the most on account of the horses which were exhausted by our long march. By Wednesday morning we had everything across the river, and were ready to resume our march.

We were then eighteen miles distant from Fort Carleton, a Hudson Bay Company's trading post on the north branch of the Saskatchewan River, which place we hoped to reach before the storm, and there find shelter for our horses. But in the afternoon a freezing north-west wind, accompanied by rain, began to blow with violence, and it was impossible to go any farther that day. Fortunately we found a place to camp well sheltered by woods. The next morning the weather was clear and magnificent, and we set out again for Fort Carleton, which we reached in the evening. But we had not to wait long for the storm. The next morning the snow fell in large flakes, and we hastened to get the horses into the stables of the fort. If we had been detained two days later the storm would have surprised us on the prairie ; we would have suffered very much and have lost our horses.

At that time, Carleton was composed of the Hudson Bay Company Fort, five or six houses inhabited by half-breeds, and a dozen Indian wigwams on the neighbouring hills. The latter were going to have their " pow-wow" during our stay ; but as I will have to describe similar scenes further on in our story, I will omit any further mention of this one.

During our stay here, nothing further of importance happened until the moment of our departure, when a romantic scene took place in our camp. A sub-constable had fallen in love with an Indian maiden. This did not at all please the Apostle of Temperance who accosted me with intense emotion, saying ; "I can't tolerate such a scandal. How I repent having enlisted in the Mounted Police." " What scandal," said I, " I don't understand you." " Do you not know," said he, that Sub-constable V. has become enamoured of an Uskinik squaw ? He wants, at any cost, to take her to Edmonton and marry her. Did you ever hear of such a disgrace ? " " I don't understand what there is about that to displease you," said I, " For my part, I don't see any inconvenience in her coming with us, if she will agree to be our cook." " Foolish man," said the Apostle of Temperance, walking away, " you are making a jest of what, to me, is a serious matter. If he takes her along, I shall go no farther."—and, in truth, we were all opposed to the project of the unhappy sub-constable. Approaching the camp I heard bursts of laughter, and, entering, I witnessed a touching and somewhat romantic scene. The poor broken-hearted lover was embracing his fiancée, bidding her a last farewell. But alas ! for the constancy of human hearts Subconstable V. soon proved the adage : " Hot love is soon cold," and his cheerful demeanour showed that with him, at least, " out of sight" meant " out of mind."

CHAPTER VIII.

AFTER the crossing of the North Saskatchewan,
which lasted three days, had been effected, and preparations made for starting the next morning, we discovered that an ox had been left on the opposite shore.
I was the cause of this neglect, for, two days previous to
crossing of the river, I had been ordered to see that the
ox-teams were safely taken over on the ferry. Therefore
it was without a murmur that I received the order from
Inspector Jarvis, to have the ox secured by daylight.
But a difficulty presented itself. How could I get across
the river which, at that place, is about 350 yards wide?
It is true there were canoes at my disposal, but I had
never handled a paddle, so I was in great perplexity,
as no time could be lost, for, as I said before, we wanted
to make an early start. After thinking for a while what
course to pursue, I remembered hearing one of our half-
breeds say that he had been for a number of years in the
service of the Hudson Bay Company, whose employees

it is well known, travel a good deal with boats when
trading with the Indians. So concluding that he could
help me in my difficulty, I went directly to him and presented my request, which was well received, and he said
that, at any time, he was at my disposal. I, therefore, went
back to my camping quarters, thinking no more about
the difficulty of crossing the river, but of finding the ox
in the morning, which, by that time, might be two or
three miles away. On this account, I passed a sleepless
night; and getting up at two o'clock in the morning, I
went to wake the half-breed, thinking we had now no
time to spare. But he was too sleepy to be disturbed at
that early hour, and he said that day-light was quite early
enough to start. Money, they say, will do anything in
this world; I tried it with him, offering him five dollars.
and a blanket besides; but they had no effect on him.
Therefore, trusting to my swimming attainments in case
of need, and being a very bright moonlight night, I made
for the river, jumped into the best canoe I could find, and
pushed away from the shore. My bold attempt was good,
so far as it went, but in a second, the current caught the
bow of the canoe, and I found myself floating rapidly
down stream, notwithstanding my utmost efforts to return to shore. Nothing daunted, I jumped into the
water, and swam back to *terra firma*, pulling the canoe
after me. Early baths of this kind are not in fashion in
the North-West, at this season of the year, but mine was
involuntary. Going to camp, I changed my clothes, and
went down to the river, ready to make another attempt

5

This time I adopted different tactics. Walking along the shore and drawing the canoe after me by means of a rope attached to the bow, I went about half a-mile up stream, thinking by that means to have more space in order to reach the landing-place on the opposite shore. Jumping in the canoe, I again set out, but encountered the same difficulties as before. Sometimes the bow would be up stream, sometimes down ; nevertheless, I kept on paddling, now right, now left, and seeing that I was making some progress gave me new hope ; and exerting all my strength, I at last reached the shore about 100 yards above the landing place.

Securing the canoe to a tree, I at once started to look for the ox ; but my endeavours were fruitless. And after rambling about till eight o'clock, I saw from a little hill where I stood, that our men were setting out from camp. I therefore concluded that the ox had been found, and returning to my canoe, which I found occupied by two Indians, I crossed with them, and making my way to the camping ground which was still occupied by a few half-breeds, I was informed by them that my conjecture was right, and that the ox had been found among the cart-oxen which had been brought over late in the evening.

The country on the left side of the North Saskatchewan, lying between Carleton and Edmonton, is of a very different nature from that we had just left. Between Qu'Appelle River and Carleton, the road was dry ; but in the region we had just entered, on account of the rains having been unusually abundant that summer, the smallest rivulets were increased to large streams, and the road, in many places, was covered with large pools of water. In these, our waggons would sometimes sink to the axles, and it required two or three ox-teams to each load to drag them through. To add to our calamity, the grass had lost its greenness by the frost, which had immediately followed the snow-storm we had experienced at Carleton.

Foreseeing these difficulties we had, it is true, purchased some barley at Carleton, to take with us for the use of our horses ; but they, not being strong enough to digest such strong food, having lived on grass alone, while travelling from the Pembina River to Carleton, were rendered ill by this diet: and some of them died. We thus had to feed the barley very sparely, and the result was that every day some of the horses would fall from hunger and fatigue. We would stop and raise them to their feet by means of poles passed beneath them, and, incredible as it may appear, I have seen those horses put immediately to work and travel on five or six miles farther.

After passing Carleton, the first station on our road was Fort Pitt, a Hudson Bay Company trading post on the North Saskatchewan. The thought of again meeting a human habitation raised our spirits, but we were soon to be disappointed in our expectations; for, when but a few miles from Fort Pitt, we came to a bifurcation of the road. The left road was the one we expected to follow ; but the other was shorter, and again joined the first mentioned a few miles beyond the fort. Inspector Jarvis took the shortest road, and, when we consider that we were then in October, we must acknowledge that he was right.

Victoria was then our next station. Our difficulties were increasing daily; the horses now were but living skeletons, and the oxen, which were of a great assistance to us, were getting weaker every day; the frost-killed grass being their only provender. Consequently our marches gradually became shorter and shorter. But in our difficulties, officers and men increased their efforts with redoubled vigour, and, at last, White Creek, about eighteen miles east of Victoria was reached. In the afternoon of the next day, some of the strongest teams were entering Victoria, while the weakest had hardly left White Creek. But the greatest harmony still reigned among us, and, as usual, the first arrived returned to assist those that had been left behind.

We had still to travel about eighty-five miles, on roads almost impassable for our heavy waggons, before reaching our destination ; and, therefore, Inspector Jarvis thought it necessary to leave five or six waggons at Victoria, and also the cows and calves, hay being scarce at Edmonton that year. This arrangement enabled him to dispose of half a dozen of men who were sent forward under the command of Sub-Inspector Gagnon with orders to make the roads passable. This was a difficult task, and often required the co-operation of all. Bridges had to be constructed over streams that were not fordable, and trunks of trees were thrown over mud holes, some of them over a hundred yards long.

As it was now near the end of October, and the weather, especially at night, getting very cold, we were losing an average of one horse a day. Yet, we would have lost more, had we not taken the precaution to stable them in tents at night.

On the 24th of this month we crossed Sturgeon Creek, which lies about twenty miles east of Edmonton, and for the next two days, we made very little progress, only reaching Horse Hills a distance of eight miles. But the road being good the rest of the distance, the men having the strongest teams were ordered to press forward as fast as possible. Thus some of them reached Edmonton that night, and the next day ; as for myself, the Apostle of Temperance and two others, we took charge of the four sick horses at Horse Hills, and walked the last twelve miles, each man holding his horse with both hands, one at the head and another at the shoulders, to keep the poor skeletons on their legs. And in this manner, we entered the gates of Fort Edmonton in the evening of the 2nd of November, the observed of all observers thereof, who never expected to see the Mounted Police arrive in such a wretched state.

We shall now go back to the main column which we left wending its way towards the junction of the rivers Bow and Belly. As already said, both water and grass were scarce on the plains that lay between Roche Percée and the junction, and therefore, it was not long before many of the horses gave out, and some of them fell to rise no more. Some of the men also began to lose courage, being so disappointed in their expectations. Constable T., especially, lost heart, and one morning applied for an interview with the Commissioner. He told Colonel French that he had enlisted in the Mounted Police, thinking there was some fighting to be done ; but that so far, the only enemy they had met was starvation, and therefore, he begged to be discharged and allowed to go home. This request greatly astonished the commander-in-chief, and no wonder, when we considered that the column was hundreds of miles from human habitation. At last, Colonel French came to the conclusion that the brain of Constable T. must be affected, and accordingly, sent for Dr. K. the surgeon. This officer came directly, and asked what was the matter. " Dr. K.," said the Commissioner, " I wish you to take charge of Constable T. whose brain, I fear, is a little affected by the moon." " What !" exclaimed Constable T, " do you take me for a fool, because I asked for my discharge ? " " What can I think of a man, who asks me without necessity for it to run to sure death ? This is what your request amounts to, but such a request I can never grant ; for, if I did, I should feel myself responsible for the disastrous results that most inevitably would ensue."

The junction was reached about the middle of September. But what a disappointment awaited them ! Instead of forts, serving as a refuge to the whiskey traders, they found only two or three roofless and deserted log shanties. On the approach of the column, the inmates of these huts had dismantled them, and fled to Uncle Sam's

Dominions, but only to return to their ignoble traffic, as soon as the Mounted Police should have retired.

The main object of the campaign having resulted in a fizzle, A. and B. divisions were ordered to set out for Edmonton. But after a half day's march, it was deemed impossible for the two divisions to reach there, on account of the weak state of the horses. Therefore, the Commissioner ordered them back, and with the whole column, he set out towards the International Boundary, dreading to be caught on the barren plains by the September snow storm. As it was, they would have been caught if the storm had come as early as in the previous year ; and in that case, both men and horses must have miserably perished ; the former from cold, having only one blanket each ; the latter from both cold and hunger.

But though the column had escaped the effect of the usual snow-storm, Colonel French was still in a great difficulty, the horses being unable to travel all the way back. But his mind was a measure set at rest at last by orders received from the Government to leave the main part of his forces in that region, if he thought it was proper to do so. The result was, that A. B. C. and F. divisions were left there under the command of Colonel McLeod, the assistant commissioner. Almost immediately a marked change for the better was visible ; for this officer, a man of giant abilities, proved himself equal to the occasion. He at once procured from Fort Benton, U. S., a good supply of food and clothing for his men, who were reduced to mere skeletons, and were almost destitute of both. As for the horses, he sent them to the Sun River Valley, U. S., to pass the winter and recruit up for the next summer's work ; and with his men, he built during the winter the fort which still bears his name.

As for Colonel French, he purchased some horses from hunters, whom he came across, and returned homeward with D and E divisions. It would take many pages of the book to relate all the hardships and sufferings they had to endure on their way. But, with clothing in tatters, and most part of the time living on half-rations, they finally passed Fort Qu'Appelle and reached Fort Pelly, at which place E division was quartered ; and which, for some time, became the headquarters of the Mounted Police, in that section of the country. Leaving this place, Colonel French resumed his march with D division towards Dufferin, and finally entered that place on the 7th of November.

Thus ended the campaign of 1874, which had it had for its theatre the European Continent would not have wanted for writers to relate its vicissitudes and perils ; yet Canadians hardly remember that eight years ago 300 volunteers offered their service to pluck from barbarism a country which, in a few years, is destined to occupy an important position on the American continent.

CHAPTER IX.

EDMONTON in 1874 was composed of only the Hudson Bay Company's fort, a Methodist church, and a few houses scattered along the banks of the river. As there were no houses to receive us, and the severity of the winter would not permit of any being built, Inspector Jarvis rented apartments within the fort itself, and thus provided shelter for the detachment.

The forts in the North-West Territories are far from being equal in solidity to those in more civilized countries. Fort Edmonton, with which we are at present concerned, consists of a palisade some twenty feet high, formed of hewn posts. At the corners of this enclosure are turrets, through the loop-holes of which can be seen the muzzles of the guns. And strange as it may appear, these slight fortifications have ever sufficed to keep at a respectful distance, even the Blackfeet Indians, so well renowned in the military annals of the United States, by the numerous massacres of which they were the authors.

Within the palisade, are situated the storehouse where

Indians exchange their furs for goods; and three parallel rows of cottages provided for the accommodation of the company's employees complete the fort. It was in these cottages that we were installed and passed the winter.

To the excitement and toil of the expedition was to succeed a monotonous and sedentary life. All we had to do was to look after the horses, and even that slight exercise grew less and less by degrees as the most of them died during the winter.

I need hardly say that this inaction was very irksome to me; for when I enlisted, it was my intention to test the accuracy of the accounts of the Indians given by novelists, and to explore those regions hitherto unknown to any but the native inhabitants. There were a few Indians near Fort Edmonton, and also at Ellice and Carleton ; but these seemed so degenerated that I resolved as soon as possible to carry out my original intention, and take a tour through the plains stretching away to the south of Edmonton, where the Indians were then said to be hunting the buffalo, and where I expected to find them in that perfectly wild and fearless state described by novelists, and pictured in my vivid imagination. I had also another motive for deciding to undertake the journey. Having heard that the buffaloes were hunted to such an extent that they would soon be exterminated, I desired to see them in their natural state while it remained in my power to do so. But the winter being very severe, I was obliged to defer my journey until March.

As it is customary in these regions to travel with dogs in the winter season, I resolved to adopt this mode of travelling myself ; and to say the least of it, this mode had for me the charm of novelty.

Accordingly, on the 5th of March, I set out with three dogs harnessed to a sled, and took the road leading to Buffalo Lake, as it was in that direction the buffaloes were said to roam. I soon found that dogs travel very well when driven by their master, but if a stranger undertakes to drive them, they not only refuse to advance, but they show their teeth in a very significant manner. The half-breed from whom I hired the team accompanied me a short distance, and then, after giving me the necessary instructions, he returned to Edmonton. But the dogs soon perceiving that their master was no longer present, stopped, and notwithstanding my urgings, would go no further. Of course, I would not yield to their caprices, but, following the advice of their owner, I fastened them firmly to a tree, and beat them unmercifully. I trust the reader will believe me when I say that it was very painful to me to be obliged to resort to such cruelty, but as far I know, it was the only means of making them go. At all events, the plan succeeded ; for, no sooner, were they released than off they went with the speed of the wind.

At night-fall, I was overtaken by a half-breed who also was going to Buffalo Lake. He proposed that we should camp together, to which I willingly agreed ; for, as neither of us had a tent, I was curious to know how my new acquaintance would prepare to pass the night. Although it was March, there was a foot of snow on the ground, and the thermometer often fell to 22° below zero. But my companion was fertile in expedients. While I was cutting some fire wood, he cleared off the snow from the spot chosen for the camp, using a tin plate, as a shovel; and a few minutes later we were melting snow to make tea and cooking some meat. The meal over, we made a large fire intended to last till morning, by the side of which we spread our blankets, and lay down to sleep. On awaking in the morning, I found my hair covered with hoar frost, but that had not hindered me from passing a very agreeable night.

After breakfast, we continued our journey, and soon came in sight of the Peace Hills. Not knowing why they were so named, I enquired of my companion. He said: "The banks of Battle River, which we shall soon reach, were formerly the site of a bloody battle between the Blackfeet Indians and the Crees; and the latter being victorious, the Blackfeet sued for peace which was concluded with great ceremony on those hills."

My companion, who was better equipped than I, and who wished to reach Buffalo Lake that same day, set out in advance. As for myself, nothing obliged me to travel fast, so I travelled on quietly, and camped that night on the shores of Red Deer Lake.

The lesson taught me by the half-breed was not lost. In a few moments, I had a large fire blazing, and, after preparing and partaking of supper, as on the previous night, I spread my blanket and soon fell into a profound sleep. During the night, however, the wolves, which are very numerous in that neighbourhood, awakened me with their doleful howls. In the spring these animals are so famished with hunger that they attack and sometimes devour even horses, if left outside. And fearing an attack I hastened to rekindle my fire, which alone could keep them at a safe distance. For even had I been armed, (which I was not, having been advised to carry no arms with me, in order to inspire the Indians with confidence), I should not have been able to withstand their attack without the aid of fire.

In the afternoon of the next day, I arrived at Buffalo Lake (so named on account of its form being similar to that of a buffalo) having travelled one hundred miles from Edmonton. On the shores of the lake was a village inhabited by Indians and half-breeds who were hunting the buffalo. The half-breed who preceded me had apprised them of my coming ; so a large party came out to meet me, each contending for the honour of entertaining an envoy of the Canadian Government.

Learning that I had come to see the buffaloes, the half-breeds assured me that they were to be found about sixty miles further south, and that it would be quite easy to satisfy my curiosity. So the following day, notwithstanding their friendly endeavours to detain me, I set out in the direction of a Cree camp situated in the valley of Red Deer River.

Before leaving Edmonton, I learned that stray buffaloes, separated from the herd, were exceedingly fierce,

and dangerous, and was advised if I met any such, to
avoid them ; and the same advice was given me by my
friendly entertainers of the previous night. To impress
this fact on my mind, one related the story of a hunter
who would never hunt on horseback ; and one day, meeting with a .buffalo bull, he fired at and wounded him, but
not severely enough to hinder him from turning upon
him. Knowing that flight could not save him from death,
the hunter threw himself flat on his face, and this stratagem saved him ; for the horns of the buffalo are so curved
and divergent, that a man so lying is out of their reach.

That afternoon my dogs suddenly stopped ; and looking round for the cause, I was not a little surprised to
see nine large buffaloes come out of a thicket and plant
themselves before me, not in the least frightened at my
presence. Satisfying themselves with a few moments' in-
spection of my appearance, they trotted off, leaving me
to pursue my journey.

The next day, I arrived at the camp, at the entrance of
which, I met an Indian who said to me in the Cree language, " my brother, the soldier, is welcome." With the
Indians, any man clothed in uniform is a soldier. I asked
him to conduct me to the wigwam of a fur-trader
whom I had previously met, and whom I knew to be in
the camp. Arriving there, the wigwam of my host was
besieged by a large number of warriors, eager to get a
glance at the Simganis (soldier) who had come to meet
them. The Indian chief (Sweet Grass) accompanied by
his counsellor and petty chiefs, came also to bid me wel-

come, and to invite me to a pow-wow (dance) which he was going to give that evening in my honour.

As a Government functionary, and besides being desirous of observing Indian habits closely, I thought it well to accept the invitation. Accordingly, after supper, accompanied by my host who acted both as guide and interpreter, I directed my steps towards the wigwam where the Council was sitting. The chief and his warriors were already assembled, and by the side of the chief a seat of furs was placed, intended for my occupation. Three Indians, each furnished with a kind of tambourine and a drum-stick, were only awaiting my arrival to strike up the music for the dance. As soon as I was seated, the squaws, old and young, entered, and the pam-pam began. And such a pantomime ! how shall I describe it ? Such shaking and balancing of the head, contortions of the face and body, such violent and uncouth movements of the arms and legs accompanied with a kind of song, interspersed with most inhuman shouts, were surely never heard and seen outside of an Indian wigwam.

As the dance went on a young Uskinik squaw approached me, and by a sign asked me to dance with her. Here was an unlooked-for turn in events. To dance as the whites do is all very well, but to dance after the Indian fashion above described, was, in my opinion, altogether too much of a good thing. But what was to be done ? All eyes were fixed upon me, seemingly anxious to know if I would dare to refuse ; for truly my manner must have indicated that I felt reluctant to accept the proffered honour. But, remembering that a refusal to dance was looked upon as an insult, I got up and taking the hand of the Uskinik squaw, did my best to imitate the ludicrous motions I had witnessed by the others. This so pleased them that the shouts and laughter was increased to a perfect uproar, and when I sat down both the chief and his warriors came to congratulate me upon my successful debut.

Tea is a favourite beverage with the Indians, and on this occasion, a great quantity had been prepared. My partner in the dance seemed to look upon my wants as her especial care, and brought a saucepan full, saying : "Miwassin, Muskakee," (here is some good medicine,) which I took, expecting to drink ordinary tea. But when I had tasted it I felt as if I had swallowed a burning coal. What had been put into the tea to make it so strong? This was a question to which I could then find no answer, but I afterwards learned that it was tobacco, and that the Indians were in the habit of brewing the weed with their tea on special occasions of rejoicing to make it intoxicating. I feared, at first, that they wanted to poison me, but seeing that all the others drank freely of it, I did the same, determined not to be outdone by any of them. About eleven o'clock I retired with my host, the fur-trader, to his wigwam ; but before going I presented the Indians with a pound of tea, with which addition to their stock of stimulants, they kept up their amusements until morning.

CHAPTER X.

An Unexpected Proposal—On the Road Again—A Disagreement—Hunting the Buffalo—Disappearance of my Guides—Visit to Another Camp—A Council of Warriors—A Peculiar Feast—On my Return—Frozen Ears—Paternal Anxiety—The Indian Doctor—Return to Buffalo Lake—Visit to the Cree Indian Headquarters—The Indian Conjuror's Account of the Creation of the World—My Return to Edmonton and Kind Reception

ON the following morning, I was about to walk out to take a view of the surroundings of the camp, when I saw the Indian Chief coming towards me, leading by the hand the young Uskinik squaw, my partner of the previous night, and followed by the counsellor and the petty chiefs. Of course I was somewhat curious to know what could be the object of this early morning visit; and to my sorrow, I soon learned what it was. Without uttering a word, the Indians walked into the wigwam and sat down. Then the chief took out a pipe and smoking a few minutes, passed it to another who followed his example, and so on, till all had smoked the pipe of peace. This done, the counsellor arose, and began to speak with remarkable vehemence and volubility. I could understand nothing of what he said but "Uskinik squaw" which he often repeated, pointing at the same time, towards the young girl. But from the countenance of my host, which

6

grew more and more gloomy as the speaker went on, and from his occasional glances at me, I could understand that, this discourse foreboded me no good. When the counsellor had ceased to speak, my host told me that the chief, as a proof and pledge of his pacific sentiments towards the whites, had resolved to give his daughter to the white man whom he considered most worthy of that honour, and that it was upon me his choice had fallen, and he now brought her to me, hoping I would fully appreciate the honour he wished to confer upon me. Honour indeed! I was terrified. My first reflections were regrets, that I had been foolish enough to venture among the Indians alone, and then, how to safely get rid of that honour. To refuse, would bring upon me imprisonment and torture, perhaps death. To marry, and desert her, I would not. To marry and live with her would be worse than death. What was I to do? I could see no way out of my difficulty, but to appear to acquiesce, that I might gain time to get away from them. So, resolving upon this course, I charged my host to say to the chief, that being neither a great warrior, nor a mighty hunter, I was far from expecting so great an honour; but, if he absolutely insisted on having me for his son-in-law, I begged for a delay of a few days in order to give my friends at Edmonton time to come and witness the wedding, adding that it was the custom among the whites, to invite many guests and to make great preparations for such an important event. My answer not only seemed to satisfy, but to greatly please the old chief; and, considering the affair settled, he arose, and with his followers retired. Congratulating myself on having escaped from such a dilemma, and for having succeeded in gaining the above respite, I felt sure of escaping them altogether.

When I had been there three days, some half-breeds arrived who were going buffalo hunting, and I set out with them. We soon came across fresh buffalo tracks, but they were so few that we thought it not worth our while to follow. So, proceeding, we reached the banks of Red Deer River about noon, and crossing, two divergent roads lay before us. My companions deliberated which one to take, but opinions were divided, words ended in contradictions, and from contradictions they were coming to blows, when I interfered, and said that fighting could do no good, as blows could not change any man's opinions. The best way would be, for each man to take the road which he thought to be the right one. My advice was followed, and, along with the larger party, I took the road to the right, and which led us to a Cree camp, at which we arrived at night-fall. These Indians had been apprised of my coming and of the object of my visit; they therefore came forth to meet me, bidding me welcome, and soon had me quartered in the wigwam of the chief, who gave a dance in honour of my arrival, similar to the one described above.

At dawn the next morning, an Indian informed me that he had seen a numerous herd of buffaloes only a mile from the camp, and that a party was going out to hunt them. This was an opportunity too good to be lost, and

therefore, having hired a horse and a rifle, I set out with
the hunters.   In order to shelter themselves from the icy
wind, the buffaloes had entered a valley surrounded by
steep hills with only a narrow passage of ingress and
egress ; and to this passage we were led by one of my travelling companions who conducted the hunt. Here a party
of the hunters was stationed, to prevent the buffaloes from
escaping, and the rest of us were dispersed in an extensive
circle, behind the hills surrounding the valley.   These arrangements completed, we ascended the hills, and, at a
given signal, simultaneously attacked the herd, both rear
and flank, the buffaloes rushing with might and main towards the only opening, and we after them.   Meeting
the fire of the party in the passage, the buffaloes turned
and charged us.   But a well sustained fire brought down
a great number of them ; and only a few succeeded in
climbing the hills and making their escape.

The hunt ended, we set to work to remove the skins
and cut up the meat.   Then, we built a fire, and roasted
what the Indians consider the choicest and most delicate
part of the buffalo, and, after enjoying this to satiety, the
meat and hides were packed on sleds brought by the
squaws for that purpose, and all returned to camp.

Being desirous of visiting the camp of Pichican, a Cree
chief, the next day and not knowing the way, I was in a
quandary as to how to accomplish my purpose, when fortunately two Indians arrived, who were sent by the Great
Chief Kiskajou (short-tail) to the principal chief of the
Blackfeet, and as they were going by the camp I wished

to visit, I asked and obtained permission to accompany them. We set out accordingly but there being no road, my dogs refused to advance. I was at a loss to know what to do, when one of the Indians signed to me to get out and follow on foot, while he led the way on snow shoes. This being done, the dogs set out again ; but the depth of the snow, and the numerous herds of buffaloes that we encountered, rendered our progress slow and difficult.

At nightfall, we encamped on the summit of a hill, a necessary precaution to prevent being trampled under foot by the buffaloes. In this bleak situation, without shelter from the wind, I expected to pass a very uncomfortable night; but being very tired and having a good fire, I slept soundly until morning. On rising, my companions were nowhere to be seen ; and not knowing what direction to proceed, I was about to retrace my steps to the camp we had left, when suddenly the Indians emerged from a snow-bank in which they had buried themselves, to protect them from the cold. This to me was a new expedient, but, I must admit, it was a good one. We then had breakfast, and thus refreshed, we set out again for the camp of Pichican, which we reached that evening.

My arrival created great surprise among the Indians, and all the greater since they had never seen a government functionary clothed in uniform. The Indians who accompanied me were assailed with innumerable questions about me, and the chief summoned a council for the following day and requested me to attend. At the ap-

pointed hour, I repaired to the council wigwam, and met
at the door a young Indian, who said to me in English :
"My brother is expected," and then conducted me to a
seat on the right hand of the chief. Being astonished to
hear an Indian speak English, I enquired where he had
learned the language, when he told me that he had spent
two years in college at Montreal, but becoming home-sick,
he had returned to his tribe, notwithstanding the entreaties of the missionary who had taken charge of his education.

In the wigwam were assembled about fifty warriors who
maintained a profound and gloomy silence which was at
length broken by the chief, who, in a solemn tone, asked
me the object of my visit. I answered that I had come
to assure myself of the correctness of the information
concerning the Indians, which I had collected from different sources, adding, that I belonged to a band of white
warriors, commissioned to protect the Indians against
their enemies. My reply was in every way satisfactory,
and immediately afterwards an Indian entered, bearing
the pipe (calumet) of peace. Having filled it with tobacco and lighted it, he handed it to the chief, who, before smoking, turned the pipe towards the four points of
the compass, to show that he was at peace with all man-
kind. Then taking a few draws, he passed the pipe to
me. I followed his example, and when the calumet had
made the tour of the assembly, two squaws entered carrying a pot of tea and a kettle of *very* young buffalo veal,
prepared with a kind of sauce. This dish the Indians

consider a great delicacy ; but to my mind it was so ob-
jectionably delicate, that had I not been afraid of dis-
pleasing my entertainers, I should have abstained from
taking any part of the feast.

When all was ready everyone stood while the chief
said grace, which was repeated by all the warriors. This
was another surprise to me, but I afterwards learned that
this tribe had become converts to Christianity, that the
chief acted as pastor to his tribe, and that, as a tribe,
they were noted for their honesty and good behaviour.

The next day (after visiting the abattoir, a kind of
enclosure formed with poles, into which the Indians drove
herds of buffalo, killing the fat ones and letting the thin
ones free), not being disposed to prolong my journey, I
bade adieu to this tribe, and set out on my return, following the same road by which we had come. I was now
without a guide, but the track of my sled in the snow
made it easy to follow the trail. Resolving to reach the
same day the camp where I had joined the buffalo hunt,
I spared neither myself nor the dogs. The day was warm,
but about sunset a cold wind set in, which at first I did
not notice, but whose baleful effects I was soon to experience, for having become exceedingly warm by the rapidity
of the march, I inadvertently raised my beaver cap, thus
exposing my ears to the freezing wind and they were
bady frozen without my realizing what had taken place.
This will not be at all surprising to those who have been
in a similar situation.

It was midnight when I arrived at the camp. After

unharnessing my dogs, I entered the wigwam of the
chief; but had scarcely seated myself near the fire when
I felt a sharp stinging sensation through my ears, and,
for the first time, discovered that they were frozen. I, at
once, resorted to the only efficacious remedy within my
reach and rubbed them well with snow. But it is useless
to attempt to describe the sufferings which I endured ;
those only who have been in similar circumstances can form
any idea of it.

As the pain became greater every moment, and the
Indians of this tribe could be of no help to me, I set out
with all speed for Edmonton, and on that afternoon arrived at the wigwam of the fur trader in Red River Camp.
The news of my arrival and misfortune spread like wild-
fire, and very soon the wigwam of my host was encum-
bered with visitors who came to sympathize with me ;
and the chief especially was so extremely anxious about
his son-in-law, that he would not leave me for a moment,
and to encourage me, said : "The great medicine man of
the nation will come to-morrow to take care of my son."
In truth, the kind old chief had sent quite a distance for
an Indian doctor, who came the next morning as the
chief had said. He seated himself in silence, with his eyes
on the ground, till the chief addressed him, and told him
why he had sent for him. Approaching me, the doctor
said, "Let my brother shew me his ears," and after a
careful examination added, "If my brother will submit
to my treatment, and follow my directions, he will soon
be healed." Then taking a root from his medicine bag,

somewhat resembling a beet, he cut some thin slices, and after chewing them till they were reduced to a pulp, he applied it to my ears; and almost immediately I felt its soothing effects. As for the plant, from which this root is produced, I am ignorant of its technical name, and I doubt if it is even known to botanists. It is called in the Cree language "Akantamoo," and grows in marshy places. Its leaves are long and curled, and the root, which tastes like a carrot, sometimes attains the length of three feet.

After a week of assiduous care and attention, my ears had so much improved that, after liberally rewarding my Doctor, I set out for Edmonton, and reached Buffalo Lake the next day. There I met some hunters who were going to the plains, but in a different direction from the one I had taken; and, postponing my return to Edmonton, I joined them.

Leaving my dogs here for a rest, I hired horses for this journey, and a march of two days brought us to the camp of the Great Chief Kiskajou. I was soon summoned by this chief, who, by the voice of his counsellor, asked me about the same questions that were asked by the chiefs I had met before. But though on this occasion I gave explanations as I did before, Kiskajou did not seem satisfied with my answers. Perhaps this was on account of my having visited his subordinates first.

While at this place, I paid a visit to the conjuror or "Wise Man" of the tribe, and asked him how he accounted for the creation of the world. He said "the Great Manito

(Spirit) had made it.   Then he made the buffalo.   But as there was no one to kill and eat the buffalo, he took some black dirt and made the Indian, and by a puff of his breath, gave him life.   Then finding the Indian required some one to wait upon him, and cook his food, the Great Manito took a piece of wood and made the squaw."

For some days, the snow had been melting rapidly, and I therefore thought it prudent to return to Edmonton as soon as possible.   Bidding adieu to the hunters and Indians, I started to Buffalo Lake which I reached in the afternoon.   I remained there till after nightfall, when, fearing the snow would melt before I reached Edmonton, I harnessed my dogs, refreshed by their rest, and started. Travelling the remainder of the night and through the next day till about three o'clock, I reached Edmonton, having covered a distance of one hundred miles with dogs and fifty miles with horses, without sleeping.

As soon as he heard of my arrival, Inspector Jarvis came to see me, and was quite surprised to find me safe and well, as various reports had reached them about me. First, that I had been frozen to death on the plains; then, that I had my feet, ears and nose frozen, and that amputation had become necessary, etc. But though I was still suffering from my frozen ears, in consequence of their having been exposed to the cold after leaving Red Deer River Camp, I was otherwise as well as I had ever been in my life.

Before taking this journey to the plains, I had expressed to Inspector Jarvis a desire to resign my position in the

Mounted Police Force; but the journey had changed my projects, and I now resolved to more thoroughly study the Indian character, and that region of the North-West which they inhabit; and by retaining my position in the Mounted Police I could more easily attain my object than by any other means.

CHAPTER XI.

ON my return from the plains, I found most of the men under arrest, and one of them suspended. This was more of the work of the Commissioner, Colonel French, who, not satisfied with the miseries already inflicted upon us, must needs add a further indignity by writing to Inspector Jarvis to select a site within twenty miles of Edmonton, on the right bank of the Saskatchewan on which he was ordered to build a Fort spacious enough to quarter two divisions; ordering that the timber should be secured by tender, but the work of building should be done by the men, and that done, we were to be set to work at farming. These instructions were received during my absence, and I therefore was not present when they were made known to the men.

I must say here that we were all very much dissatisfied with having been obliged, at outrageous prices, to purchase our clothing from the Hudson Bay Company's store with

our own money, no provision having been made by the
Commissioner for renewing our stock of clothing when
needed ; and this, with many other circumstances, caused
the men upon receiving the order to go to farming, to reply that they did not enlist in the Mounted Police for
that purpose, and they could have done that kind of work
without coming so far.

Under these circumstances Inspector Jarvis acted as
becomes a good officer. He could not disobey the orders
of his superior without dishonouring himself, and was
therefore obliged to put the refractory men under arrest,
and suspend their leader until the arrival of Colonel
French, who alone had power to try their case and inflict
punishment.

In accordance with instructions received, Inspector Jarvis removed his men in the spring of 1875 to a site on
the south bank of the river, eighteen miles from Edmonton, and began at once to build Fort Saskatchewan, promising the men fifteen cents a day extra pay.   But no farming work was undertaken that summer.   There were, at
that time, only two or three temporary cabins in that
neighbourhood, occupied by gold finders ; but since then a
marvellous change has taken place.   The country around
Fort Saskatchewan is exceedingly fertile and a great
number of colonists have settled there and successfully
till the soil.   On the opposite bank of the river extends a
valley some three miles in length, where elegant houses
are to be seen, about which rises the Roman Catholic
Chapel of *Notre Dame de Lourdes*; and from three miles

above the chapel to four miles below it, as far as the mouth of Sturgeon Creek, the banks of the Saskatchewan are occupied by settlers.

In the fall of 1875, Colonel French, to the great joy of almost every member of the Mounted Police, resigned his commission; and he did so, just in time to save the Government the trouble of dismissing him. Colonel McLeod, the Assistant Commissioner, whose proficiency we have already related, was appointed in his place. This officer came to Fort Saskatchewan in the spring of '76. He called us all together, released the men under arrest, and said that he was very sorry when he heard that men who had so willingly accomplished feats almost unparalleled in history, had revolted for so trifling a cause. He had no desire to excuse the doings of his predecessor, far from it, but his mistakes were not just grounds for revolting; and as obedience was the first condition of military discipline, nothing like order could exist without it. He ended by saying that the past would be forgotten, and he hoped, that as long as he remained Commissioner, his orders would be of such a nature that no man would feel inclined to disobey. And I may here add, that his hopes were fulfilled; for during the whole of the time that he remained in office, not a murmur was heard, and all were proud of having such a leader.

In the account of my first journey to the plains, we have seen that in the region of Red Deer River, buffaloes were very numerous; and here the Indians during the winter season hunt them. To protect these Indians from the whiskey traders, Tail Creek Fort was built about half-way between Fort Calgarry, on Bow River, and Fort Saskatchewan. This fort was built near the mouth of Tail Creek, and a part of the division was quartered there.

·In August, '76, Sub-constable M. and myself, were ordered to hold ourselves in readiness to start for Tail Creek, where we were to pass the winter; and for my part, I was delighted with the prospect of a second sojourn among the Indians. This time as I was not to spend a few weeks only, but a few months in their company, it would afford me an excellent opportunity of studying their manners and customs.

After my journey to the plains the previous year, I should have been able myself to pilot the way to our destination; but for greater security Constable C., who had been to Tail Creek several times, was detailed to go with us, as guide.

At ten o'clock in the morning of the 25th of August, we set out, following the road which passes along parallel to the right bank of the Saskatchewan, but at some distance from it, and which leads to a gristmill situated about opposite Fort Edmonton. We were about one hundred and twenty miles from Tail Creek, but having four spirited horses, we expected to accomplish the journey in five days at the most.

There was certainly a striking contrast between my two travelling companions. Sub-Constable M. was a Scotchman, seldom offered a remark, and answered questions only after mature deliberation. But quite the contrary was Constable C., who was an Irishman, and boasted of his descent from the ancient Irish kings. He was never quiet and never tired of admiring the vast prairies that were stretching before us, frequently reminding us of the thousands of labourers, who were living in large towns in the most abject misery, and who, if they were settled here, where land cost nothing and never becomes exhausted, would think themselves the happiest of men.

We were then traversing one of the most beautiful and fertile regions of the North-west. On our right, in a deep bed, rolled the majestic waters of the Saskatchewan. According as we recede from the river bank, the ground gradually rises as far as the Beaver Hills which lie between Edmonton and Fort Saskatchewan, in the direction parallel to the river. The soil enclosed between the hills is very fertile; timber suitable for building is plentiful, and game very abundant.

As for the road we were following, the settlers had abandoned it for that which extends along the left branch of the river. We had not taken the last, in order to avoid crossing the river at Fort Saskatchewan and Edmonton. However, it would have been better to have chosen this road rather than the first, which being covered with luxuriant grass, was difficult to follow.

At sunset, being yet several miles from the mill, we camped on the banks of a brook that we had just crossed. Scarcely had we set our horses at liberty to graze, when

Constable C., taking possession of the kettles, ran to fill them with water for the supper; a few minutes after, a large fire was burning and soon the repast was served on the grass. Neither I nor Sub-constable M. could understand the reason of so much haste, and to our questions Constable C. would reply briefly, "hurry up." Our supper was nearly over, when an Indian, issuing from a neighbouring thicket, came towards us. He was the chief of the tribe, dwelling among the Beaver Hills. . After shaking hands with us, the only mode of salutation used among the Indians, he seated himself, without restraint, beside the kettles: his hair waving, and having for a dress nothing but a " pagne."

At the sight of such "sans gène" Sub-Constable M. made a grimace, and but for Constable C., who made him a sign not to stir, he was about to rush upon the Indian, and make him decamp. It was well for us that he did not do so, for six other Indians who just then were approaching, followed by their squaws and papooses, would have quickly resented any insult offered to their chief. All sat down around the kettles, waiting for the remains of our meal, and the scene suggested a picture worthy of the greatest painter.

"Do you understand now," said Constable C., "my hurry in preparing supper? We shall have to do thus every time we camp in the neighbourhood of Indians, and I hope we shall have time to eat before they arrive; for the sight of their persons takes away all my relish for food."

7

After having scraped and even licked our kettles, the Indians smoked for awhile, and then held a council. On hearing them repeat the word *neemito*, which in the Cree language signifies "to dance," I understood that they were about to engage in that exercise. The chief addressed a few words to an Uskinik squaw, who complying with his request, bounded away with the rapidity of a deer. At the end of an hour, she returned, holding in her hand a tambourine and a drum stick which she gave to one of the Indians, who, after tuning the instrument, began the pam-pam already known to the readers. We have already described a similar dance ; so we need not return to it. Sub-constable M. and I were not in a humour to take part in it, but Constable C., whom a trifle interested, danced the whole night.

The next day, in order to escape the importunities of the Indians, we set out before breakfast and soon arrived at a bifurcation of the road. On the left bank of the Saskatchewan, were to be seen some houses which, according to Constable C., formed a part of the colony of Edmonton. We were then near the creek upon which is built the mill where the road to the right terminates. As we had to cross this creek about a mile above the mill, we took the left hand road : but, after marching on it for some time, we remarked that it was taking us away from the direction we had to go. So, retracing our steps to the bifurcation, we took the other way and soon came to another branch of the road from which place appeared on our right the grist mill and Fort Edmonton. Taking the road to the left, which, being recently laid out, was scarcely passable, we soon arrived on the banks of the creek where we expected to cross on a bridge which had been built some time during the previous year. But we were disappointed in our expectations ; the bridge had been carried away by a flood in the spring. The stream being not fordable, we had to build a bridge. But it will be said, does not such a work require weeks and even months ? By no means, a few hours were sufficient to throw across the creek a temporary bridge. While my comrades were cutting some branches, I cut down two or three trees which fell across the stream. Upon the trunks were laid the branches which were covered with earth. This done, we safely crossed to the other side. Resuming our march, we were soon on the road from Edmonton to . Buffalo Lake, the same one that I had taken the preceding year, and which we were to follow as far as the vicinity of the above lake.

Although my journey to the plains had been made when the ground was covered with snow, this road was pretty familiar to me, on account of certain striking incidents which occurred on it. Here is the place where the half-breed, from whom I had hired a team of dogs, gave me his last instructions ; a little farther, the tree to which I had fastened the dogs to give them a beating, etc., etc.

Towards evening, we reached White Mud Creek, a tributary of the Saskatchewan, about ten miles distant from Edmonton, on the banks of which we camped for the night. We would have halted sooner but for some

Indian families which we overtook and left behind us.
We had taken with us only six days provisions, hence,
notwithstanding the good will of Constable C., we could
not invite Indians to our meals. Besides, Sub-constable
M., by his grimaces, showed his want of sympathy with
such guests. At nightfall, the next day, we met, near
Pipestone Creek, the interpreter of the Mounted Police
from Fort McLeod, greatly excited by fear. Bearing dis-
patches for Fort Saskatchewan, he informed us of the
massacre of the American General Custer and his army
by the Sioux ; adding, that the Indians of Canada were
secretly arming themselves, and would soon fall unexpectedly upon the whites and half-breeds. The check received by the Americans was not very serious. Custer
had under his command only three or four hundred soldiers, a very feeble force when we consider that he was
attacked in an unfavourable position by several thousand
savages. In the open country, notwithstanding its inferi-
ority of number, Custer's army would have easily gained
the day. The Indian extraction of the interpreter will
account for his fears ; for the half-breeds, like the Indians,
are not remarkable for their courage. The following
anecdote, which I have from a reliable source, will give an
idea of their courage, or rather their want of courage.

"One day a great number of mounted half-breeds, accompanied by carts, were going to hunt buffaloes. Among
them was a French Canadian, who, not being able to ride,
was placed in a cart. After marching a long time without meeting any game, they arrived in the territory of

the Blackfeet who were the terror of the half-breeds. (This was a fact which had been verified in 1874 ; for before the arrival of the Mounted Police they had but rarely ventured beyond the territory of the Crees.) As their provisions were almost exhausted, and by retracing their steps starvation was awaiting them, they advanced carefully, determined to beat a retreat as soon as they should perceive the Blackfeet. During two days they met nobody, but the third day, just as they resumed their journey, they perceived in the distance some horsemen coming towards them. Although superior in numbers, they were seized with such terror that before assuring themselves as to whether they had to deal with friends or enemies, they took to flight, abandoning the carts and the Canadian, who besought them, but in vain, to remain. These Indians were Crees, and seeing nobody on the carts they were preparing to take possession of them when they perceived the Canadian standing up, curious to know who the newcomers were. The Crees, who, like the hare in La Fontaine's fable, thought themselves valiant warriors, haughtily asked him why his companions had run away. When they learned the reason of it they burst out laughing, and called the half-breeds cowards. The latter had concealed themselves in a low place, at some distance from where they could see without being seen, and seeing that the Canadian was unmolested and continuing his journey with the carts, they issued from their hiding place and soon overtook him, ashamed of having shown so little courage."

The next morning at daybreak, the interpreter, whose nerves had been steadied by sleep, set out again, and very soon after we did the same. Having come to a bifurcation of the road, I remarked to Constable C., who took the road to the right, that the road to the left seemed to me to be the one I had followed the preceding year. However, I did not insist, when he assured me that we were in the right way. Meanwhile, I was asking myself, but in vain, to what destination the other road, which was much travelled, could lead. After crossing Pipe Stone Creek we entered a bushy region, and as we gradually advanced the road became less passable and turned in a westerly direction. We could not, therefore, be on the right road, as the way from Edmonton to Buffalo Lake lies in a southern direction and across what may be called a prairie country. I communicated my fears to Constable C. and asked him if he was perfectly sure that we were on the right road. He was forced to admit that he now entertained some doubt about it, but he thought that we would probably reach Battle River by that road at all events, and by following the banks of that stream it would be easy for us to find our way again. In expecting that we would reach Battle River he was greatly mistaken, since instead of going south, we were going west as before stated, and admitting even that we should reach Battle River that way, how did he know that we could travel along its banks with the cart? We were travelling at random, as we shall see later on.

The next day, at noon, we arrived on the banks of a stream which we crossed, after demolishing a beaver dam which obstructed the way, and, entering a region where the grass was abundant and the soil loamy (different in that respect to the region we had just left, in which the soil is very sandy), we resolved to remain until the next day in order to allow our horses time to recuperate. As the soil where we stood is of the same nature as in the vicinity of Battle River, Constable C. assured me once more that we would soon be on the banks of that stream. He especially said this in order to raise the spirits of Sub-constable M. who, having charge of the provisions, had told us that we had hardly enough flour to last two days. Whether there was any flour or not, it mattered little to Constable C. who, being a dead shot and having with him a fowling piece, expected to bring down all the game that would come within range. Unfortunately since leaving Fort Saskatchewan, we had not met any game, and if this continued, his skill would be of little service to us. I was, however, far from becoming discouraged, for in case the flour and the game would fail, I counted upon attacking two hundred pounds of bacon that were in the cart.

Very early the next morning, while Sub-constable M. was preparing breakfast, I went to look after the horses in order to bring them in. But notwithstanding a careful search of two hours, I came back with only two horses to my travelling companions. "Very probably" said Constable C. to me, "we shall soon find the horses, meanwhile put one of the remaining horses in the cart and go forward till you reach Battle River. As we shall travel quicker than you, we shall soon overtake you." His excessive confidence caused me to smile; but I set out nevertheless, in advance, urging the horse forward, anxious as I was to arrive *somewhere*. The more I advanced the more difficult became the road, which was narrow, and in a good many places, obstructed with stumps and felled trees. As I said before, the road to Buffalo Lake that we should have followed, passes through scarcely anything but plains; the road on which I was travelling was becoming more and more hilly, and the forest more dense.

Having marched up a gradual ascent for an hour or so, I suddenly found myself on the verge of a very steep descent. Too late to stop the horse, and the cart not being provided with a brake, I found myself going down hill with extreme velocity. This unrestrained course could not last very long, and arriving at a turn of the road, the cart upset and I was thrown, head first, to a great distance. This fall stunned me for a moment, and on recovering my senses, I saw the horse lying on his back, and struggling in the harness. To set him at liberty was the work of a second, and I ascertained with pleasure that he had only some slight bruises. As I was about to unload the cart in order to raise it again, I heard a hollow roaring, similar to that produced by waves breaking against the rocks. At first, I thought it was the waving of the trees agitated by the wind; but the noise being heard only in front of me, I soon concluded that it was produced by some other cause. Leaving the cart there, and followed by the horse, which I could not leave alone in this unknown region, I set forward in the direction of the noise. After walking in that manner some hundred yards, I came in sight of a lake on the shore of which at some distance to the right, were a few log cabins. The lake was rough, and the noise that I had heard was produced by the dashing of the waves against its rocky shore. But what lake was it? This was a question that I could not answer. After reflecting for a while, I remembered that, since we went astray, we had been marching in a southwestern direction; and, as Pigeon Lake lay that way, I concluded that it was that large sheet of water which I saw before me. It was then useless to go any farther; so, I immediately returned to the cart, from which I removed the baggage and set it up again. Then I hitched the horse in order to retrace my steps. While turning around, I heard the gallop of a horse which was approaching, and a few moments afterwards, Constable C. appeared, mounted on his horse, which was pouring with sweat, and whose sides were lacerated by the spurs of its rider. Constable C. was so excited that one would have thought that he had been running for life. "Do you know where we are?" said he, at length. "Certainly," said I, "I cannot so soon forget that we are on the banks of Battle River; only, to effect a crossing of several miles, a ferry is absolutely necessary. Don't you think it would be better to return, and cross

Battle River where it is fordable ?"   " Pray cease your raillery," he replied, " like you, I want to go back, but first try and answer my question."   " My answer will perhaps surprise you," said I, " but if you desire it, I tell you that we are at this moment in the forest that surrounds Pigeon Lake." "That is what I have just learned from a settler," said he, "on hearing this, I put my horse to a gallop in the hope of sparing you a useless march, but I was too late to overtake you before your arrival at the lake."

Notwithstanding our critical situation, Constable C. soon recovered his usual gaiety, feeling confident that two Indians which he had hired would find the lost horses.   In the evening we met Sub-constable M. and camped about ten miles from the Lake.

CHAPTER XII.

PIGEON LAKE is about ten miles distant from the Saskatchewan River and fifty miles from Edmonton. In round numbers, it is about fifteen miles long and ten miles. wide. Upon its shores, there is a colony, whose inhabitants, chiefly Indians and half-breeds, live by hunting and fishing. This lake abounds in fish ; and the settlers around Edmonton and Fort Saskatchewan often go to Pigeon Lake in autumn to exchange goods for fish with the Indians and half-breeds. In the vicinity of the lake, the soil is fertile, and the settlers there cultivate vegetables and a few cereals. But on account of the high price of labour, the clearing of the land would entail too great an expense to permit the cultivation of cereals being undertaken on a large scale. It is from Pigeon Lake and two other lakes situated farther south, that Battle River takes its rise.

Next morning, the Indians brought us the horses we had lost. We congratulated ourselves on getting out of the predicament so cheaply, when we remembered that horses lost in similar circumstances, have often been found only after months aud even years of most careful search.゚

Before resuming our journey, we exchanged with a settler some bacon for dry meat. It may be well to make known to the reader the process by which the Indians prepare this kind of meat.

Buffalo and deer are the kind of animals the most suitable for furnishing dry meat, which is generally prepared in summer time. After having killed and skinned the game, it is cut into large thin slices which are dried in the sun. This meat thus becomes very hard, and, protected from moisture, it resists decomposition. The Indians employ the same process to preserve fish.

He who buys meat and fish thus prepared, from the Indians, for his own use, must not be very fastidious as to cleanliness. I have often seen Indian and half-breed families trample with their bare feet upon the dry meat intended for sale. In order to be easily eaten, dry meat ought to undergo a long preparation; but when travelling, as time is limited, it is often eaten without being prepared, and in such a case good teeth are necessary.

Although travelling rapidly, it was only in the afternoon of the next day that we reached the road leading to Buffalo Lake; and the horses being tired, we camped early between the two Pipestone Creeks.

To my travelling companions who had good teeth, it was indifferent whether the meat was tender or not; but as for me, it was otherwise, I was suffering so much from

my teeth that I could hardly eat any of it. My friends
were very much concerned about this, and asked themselves, how I would be able to live until our arrival at
Tail Creek. I calmed their fears, saying that I would be
able to manage very well for two or three days. After
supper, to their great surprise, I drew from the cart, a
large piece of bacon which I cut into small slices. They
watched me without saying anything, wondering what I
intended to do with it. Then I put the bacon in the
kettle which I filled up with water and placed on the
fire. "What are you doing there?" said Constable C·
"I am cooking some bacon," I answered. "Do you know
what you are doing, foolish man? If you eat all that
salt meat, you will not find water enough to quench your
thirst," said he.

"Never you mind, I shall not drink more than usual,"
said I. "My meat will be preferable to yours, which to
my mind, resembles parchment more than meat." I
rendered the bacon less salt by several times renewing
the water in the kettle, and allowed it to cook well.
When it had cooled, I gave some of it to my friends to
taste, and they acknowledged that bacon thus prepared
was not very salt, and consequently preferable to dry
meat.

About ten o'clock the following morning, we reached
Peace Hills. From here, a slightly sloping plain extends
as far as Battle River. This region, which is exceedingly
fertile, is yet almost uninhabitated. The reason of this
is that settlers who go to the North-West, find fertile

lands without going so far. But the Battle River region will not long remain unoccupied, for it will soon be completely transformed by the emigrants which will flock there when the Pacific Railroad which will pass through or near it is completed.

In the afternoon we crossed Battle River, and, at nightfall, we reached Red Deer Lake, near the shore of which we pitched our tent for the night. Considering its little depth, this lake is in reality only a large pond ; and, at that time, being covered with ducks, Constable C. thought he would have rare sport, and, at the same time, add to our stock of provisions. Accordingly, he set out at once ; but he burn't his powder to no purpose, the game remaining beyond the range of his gun.

Being then only about thirty miles from Tail Creek, we set out early the next day, in hope of reaching our destination before night. A little before noon, we came to a bifurcation, from which Buffalo Lake was presented to our view. The road to the left was the same that I had followed the preceding year, and the road to the right, which goes by Tail Creek, was the one we had now to travel. This route being entirely unknown to me, it fell to Constable C.'s lot to act again as guide ; but he was no more successful than in the first place, for, as we went along, we came to so many bifurcations that we went astray three times, losing thus so much time, that it was midnight, when we arrived at the hills that overlook Fort Tail Creek. As we had to descend a very steep hill, and the night being very dark, Sub-constable M. suggested that we should leave the cart there until morning, and proceed to the Fort with the horses. But Constable C. who, I must say, was full of expedients, and was acquainted with the road, tied the wheels of the cart by means of ropes in order to prevent them from turning; and, in that manner, we reached the valley without accident. Very soon after, we were knocking at the gate of the Fort; and the men in charge there, who were in bed, hearing our calls, got up and let us in, being much pleased at our arrival. What followed next was an abundant repast which they quickly prepared, and which caused us to forget our recent privations.

Fort Tail Creek was then occupied by four men, one of them, Constable P. being in charge of the detachment. Having enlisted in the Mounted Police in 1873, he distinguished himself during the campaign of 1874, and his skill in buffalo-hunting added to his reputation, and caused him to be surnamed " Buffalo Slayer." He was a man twenty-five years of age. His high stature and stoutness denoted herculean strength, and his piercing eye and martial appearance gave him an air of command that I shall never forget. After questioning us about Fort Saskatchewan, he began to extol the region about Tail Creek. But for my part, I could not see what there was to extol, as it resembled a desert. However, Constable P did not stop there; from the geography of Red Deer River he passed suddenly to the brilliant future in store for the North-West. He gave a minute description of the principal agricultural and manufacturing machines then in

existence, and sketched with extraordinary clearness the
lives of their inventors. From the applied sciences he
passed rapidly to the exact sciences, and from practice to
theory. In short, Constable P. held us entranced for two
hours by his reasoning, and his strong and eloquent
voice.

This long and learned dissertation, to which my companions listened with open mouth, had astonished me. I
could not undertand how such a young brain could contain so much knowledge, and asked myself why this
"science vivante" had come to exile himself in the North-
West. This was a mystery, and, feeling myself invisibly
attracted by this wonderful man, I resolved to solve
the mystery. Therefore, after many fruitless attempts to
sleep, I got up early in the morning and directed my steps
towards his quarters ; but seeing that he was yet in bed,
I went to visit the neighbourhood while awaiting his
awakening.

Fort Tail Creek consists of three buildings only,
whose walls are made of logs placed one above another,
and the roofs formed of poles covered with hay and earth.
When these roofs have not sufficient pitch, the rain easily
penetrates them. Two of these buildings (one used for
men's quarters and the other for a stable) are surrounded
by a stockade made of stakes. As for the third house, it
was the dwelling of the constable or the officer, as the
case might be, in charge of the forts. Situated in a bushy
valley, Fort Tail Creek is overlooked by hills covered
with fir trees. On the right, flows Red Deer River, on

the left, Tail Creek.   But the site is not a good one ; for, in time of war, the surrounding hills would afford a refuge, and protection to the enemy.

After a long walk I returned to the Fort, and thinking that our savant was up, I turned my steps towards his house, the door of which I found open.   He was not within, and I thought that, like me, he had gone for a walk.   I was about to retrace my steps, when, on a shelf, I saw a row of books, and, being curious to inspect the works of Constable P., I entered, thinking that the scarcity of books in the North-West would justify the liberty I took.   While I was engaged in glancing through the books, which for the most part dealt with mathematical, physical, and natural sciences, Constable P. returned, and, without waiting for any explanation about my intrusion in his house, he took a seat and sat down with an air of complete satisfaction, inviting me to do the same.

" Sub-constable D.," said he after a pause, " you cannot imagine how glad I am that you have come here.   I am, at present, engaged in very important scientific studies, and your competency in those matters will be of great service to me."

" It is a mistake," I replied, " if you have been told that I ———— "

" Hear me to the end," said he.   " This morning I went to your place to ask you what day we could begin together our scientific studies.   I was informed that you were out ; but here you are at last, and I now propose to you my project, do you accept it ? "   " I cannot," said I,

8

"for the very reason that the subjects you propose to study are beyond my reach. What brings me here is the desire of gaining from your society the knowledge of which you gave us a general idea last night." "What is that?" said he. "It is you that will be the teacher and I the student."

I thought, at first, that Constable P. was only jesting, but seeing that he was resolved to study, I concluded that he was making a serious proposal.

"I have," said he, "deeply studied geometry and the other elementary mathematical sciences ; but convinced that, in order to build a house, it is necessary to lay a solid foundation, I am of the opinion that we should begin at the beginning."

"Let it be well understood," said I, "that I am your pupil ; on this condition only I accept your offer. However, if my very limited knowledge of those subjects can be of use to you, I am at your disposal ; but I prefer receiving lessons to giving them."

The lessons being arranged, I departed, promising to return in the evening. That day, time glided very slowly for me, hours appeared days, for I was anxious to see how such a scholar would handle the propositions of geometry. The time appointed for the lessons came at last, and I repaired to the house of Constable P., who appeared meantime to have reviewed the lessons.

"Well," said he, "let us begin with geometry." He enunciated the first proposition in plane geometry, and then passed to the demonstration which he uttered with great volubility, but of which I understood nothing. At my request, he repeated the demonstration as many as three times, but at the end, I was no more advanced than at the beginning.

"I am really disappointed," said he, "that you do not understand. Let us go on with the second proposition."

It was the same with the second as with the first—I understood nothing; and at that moment, having yet no doubt about the scientific ability of Constable P. I concluded that he had a way of reasoning that a common man could not follow. As we went daily on with our studies, I gradually began to think that his knowledge of the subjects on which he was discoursing with so much volubility was very superficial; but I had then no time to verify it, as he received orders to repair at once to Fort McLeod. I had forgotten him, when, a year afterwards, he wrote me a letter, reminding me of our studies at Tail Creek, and proposing that we should continue them by correspondence. In order to be agreeable, as well as to clear up my doubts concerning his scientific attainments, I accepted. He answered me by the next mail, sending me absurd solutions of problems, and ridiculous questions. I had, therefore, to give up corresponding with this savant, comprehensible only to those whose brains have lost their balance.

CHAPTER XIII.

Constable P. is Succeeded by Constable S., of Fort Saskatchewan—Winter
  Dwelling of Buffalo Hunters—State of the Region between the Rivers Bow
  and Red Deer during the Winter—Sad fate of a Courageous Missionary—
  Inquest of a Supposed Murder perpetrated at Tail Creek—My Return to
  Fort Saskatchewan.

CONSTABLE P. was succeeded by Constable S., of Fort Saskatchewan. He had not, like his predecessor, the mathematical fever, but he was a good non-commissioned officer, and ever mindful of the duties he had to fulfil.

In the North-West Territories the autumn is by far the most pleasant season of the year. The temperature is mild, and with the exception of the infallible snow-storm of September, there is really no bad weather. As this is the most favourable season for travelling, and the surroundings of Tail Creek were very solitary, we frequently made excursions to the plains which afforded us very agreeable recreation.

About the middle of October the Indian and half-breed hunters began to arrive; the former having no carts but using their squaws (whom they load like wild beasts of burden), their horses and dogs to transport their baggage; as for the half-breeds, they carried their luggage in Red

River carts, and as many of them had been there the previous year their cabins were ready to receive them, and
they had only to take their goods in and settle down ; but
the new comers had to build, and this is the way they set
about it : Selecting a site well sheltered from the wind,
and amply supplied with wood and water, they felled
some trees, and placing the trunks one above another,
formed the walls of the new building. The roof was constructed with poles placed in rows and covered with hay
and earth. Holes were cut in the walls for door and windows, the latter being closed in when so required with
the skins of animals ; while the doors were made of slabs
of wood split with the axe and fastened together with
thongs of rawhide. The chimney was constructed with
unburned bricks composed of hay and mud, and the floor
formed of hewed logs completed the carpenter work.
This done, they plastered the crevices well with mud and
the cabin was ready for occupation. The ease with which
they are constructed, and the wanderings of game, will
account for the number of these cabins to be found
throughout the whole North-West.

The surroundings of Fort Tail Creek were soon occupied by three or four hundred persons, and night was
made hideous by the deafening cries and repeated pow-
wows of the Indians and the no less discordant screeches
of the violins of the half-breeds, who vied with the
Indians in turning our hitherto peaceful valley into a
very bedlam.

Winter came at last in all its rigour, and snow fell in abundance early in November. Then followed the storms common in those regions and which usually arose very suddenly,—so suddenly indeed, that the bands of hunters roaming over the plains in search of buffalo were often in danger of being overcome before reaching shelter. The following episode will illustrate what not unfrequently occurs :—

Some six years ago, a missionary named McDougal, who had resided in that country for about twenty-five years, started to visit an Indian camp about twenty miles distant, and which he expected to reach the same day. Mounted on his best horse, he yet could proceed but slowly, as the snow was a foot deep and he had no track to guide him. He had, however, advanced several miles when suddenly the wind arose, the sky became overcast with clouds, and in less time than it takes to write the fact the darkness of midnight and a blinding snow-storm of indescribable violence was upon him.

Unable to see his way, he wandered at random, and, at last, overcome with the cold, he lost control of himself entirely, fell from his horse and was soon overcome by that fatal sleep which knows no awaking. The return of the horse which, instinctively found his way to his own stable, gave the alarm, and only after the most diligent search by the Indians, was the body of this unfortunate missionary recovered.

Our sojourn at Tail Creek was gliding slowly and mon- otonously by, when an event occurred which produced a great sensation in our little colony. A report was circulated that a half-breed woman had murdered her foster child. Constable S. immediately instituted an inquest, and, as I spoke English and French, I was instructed to bring all the inhabitants to the Fort. A difficult task, the reader will say, and so I thought at first ; but, going about my work with calm assurance, I was surprised to find that both half-breeds and Indians would follow me like so many sheep.

The inquest was prosecuted rigorously for two days, but no evidence whatever could be produced to criminate the woman ; and we were forced to the conclusion that the report was a calumny, which had for its origin a malignant supposition which, passing from mouth to mouth, had grown to such huge dimensions as to make the unfortunate woman appear a murderer.

In the month of March, 1877, I had orders to return to Fort Saskatchewan ; and as the melting snow rendered the roads difficult for horses to travel, Constable T., at the expense of the Government, hired a dog-team by which I was to be conveyed to Battle River, and from whence a similar team was to take me on to Edmonton.

The time appointed for my departure was midnight, as the snow would be hardened by the night-frost, and, punctual to the time, the half-breed, who was the best runner on Tail Creek, arrived at the Fort. I took my seat on the sled, and we started at full speed.

As runners, the half-breeds consider themselves superior to the whites ; and after having proceeded about five miles, feeling somewhat chilled, I thought I would warm myself, and put the speed of my driver to the test at the same time. So, jumping out of the sled, I gave the dogs a few lashes with the whip, and away they went at a gallop, leaving us far in the rear. We ran on and on, until the half-breed could continue no longer, but taking advantage of a bend in the road, he ran across the prairie and in that way got in front of the dogs. Jumping into the sled, he put whip to the dogs, leaving me to make my way as best I could. Redoubling my speed, I ran for a mile or two, and finally, the dogs slackening their speed, I overtook them, and getting into the sled, rode to Battle River which we reached at sunrise. Discharging my man, I hired another team, and set out for Edmonton that afternoon, and travelling on through the night, I arrived there about three o'clock in the morning. Here, taking a short rest, I set out for Fort Saskatchewan, and finally reached there the same day.

CHAPTER XIV.

THE quartering of A Division at Fort Saskatchewan, had the good effect of maintaining order throughout the whole region comprised between Victoria and the Rocky Mountains, in one direction, and the rivers Bow and Peace in the other. From the year 1875 to 1879, several arrests were made, chiefly among the Indians ; and some of them were guilty of the most heinous crimes, Among the number were four murderers. Two of these murderers were arrested in 1877, but died in prison without being tried for their crimes. The third was a cannibal, who had killed and eaten his wife and children, and the fourth, a father who had murdered his son.

An eyewitness of the execution of the cannibal, the first that had taken place in the North-West, I will here relate the story of his most horrible crime, his arrest, treatment, confession, and execution.

Kakisikutchin (a Cree word signifying "swift runner") was the name of the cannibal. In the autumn of 1878, with his wife and children, he repaired to the left bank

of Sturgeon Creek that he might hunt in that neighbourhood during the winter. His efforts were successful, and
therefore there was no real cause for his crime. The
only way we can account for it is this : Acts of canni-
balism are said to be of frequent occurrence in the Polar
Regions. When game cannot be found, the Indians are
first driven to it by want, and after having once tasted
human flesh, an irresistible, desire follows to eat it again.
Probably Kakisikutchin was one of this class, for with
abundance of provisions in the wigwam, and without
provocation, he first slew and ate his youngest child, then
the rest of his children in turn, and finally his wife met
the same fate. In the spring of 1879, he returned to his
tribe at Egg Lake, and, surprised at seeing him return
alone, he was asked what had become of his wife and
children. From his evasive answers they concluded a
crime must have been committed, and they imparted their
fears to Inspector Jarvis who caused him to be arrested
and imprisoned at Fort Saskatchewan. An inquest was
instituted, and the remains of the victims discovered.
Though the Indian had at first denied his guilt, when
confronted with their remains, he confessed. His crime
so exasperated the Indians that they resolved to destroy the murderer, if he succeeded in escaping justice at
the hand of the law.

On the 8th of August a competent jury declared Kakisikutchin guilty, and Lieut.-Colonel Richardson, a sti-
pendiary magistrate, sentenced him to be hung on the
20th of December. The prisoner, who heard his sentence

with apparent indifference, having declared himself a Roman Catholic, a priest was sent for who, by his constant and assiduous attention, succeeded in bringing about a great change in the mind of the condemned.

On the day before the execution took place a gallows was erected within the Fort, the rope tested, and everything made in readiness. The priest passed the whole night with the condemned, and also breakfasted with him. Finally the Sheriff, attended by Inspector Jarvis and the executioner, entered the jail and announced to the prisoner that his hour had come. The executioner tied his hands, the guards entered and conducted him to the scaffold, attended by the priest and the officers. Being placed on the trap, the opportunity was given him to address the large crowd which had gathered to witness the execution. After saying a few words, in which he again acknowledged his guilt and thanked those who had charge of him during his incarceration for their uniform kindness, the bolt was drawn and Kakisikutchin launched into eternity.

When one has contributed in any degree towards the formation of a town or village it is with regret that one leaves it.

After having spent three years in the North-West I first thought of returning to Ontario, but when opportunities for departure presented themselves I found myself without the courage to carry out my resolution. Thus postponing my departure from time to time, the year 1880 found me still at Fort Saskatchewan ; and in consequence of this repeated postponement, when I spoke of returning to France in the spring of this year no one thought me in earnest ; nevertheless I was firmly resolved to do so ; though an unexpected accident, the account of which I shall presently give, caused me to delay my departure much longer than I had intended,

In February of this year I was invited to attend a play and ball given by the inhabitants of Edmonton. My readers will naturally ask how, in a wild country like this, theatrical representations could be given. Nevertheless these plays are of frequent occurrence, and this is how the matter is arranged.

First, a managing committee is formed, whose duty it is to make all necessary preparations, and to invite the guests. Invitations are frequently sent to a distance of fifty miles, and thus the guests are sometimes reckoned by hundreds. As these balls sometimes last five or six days, an abundance of provisions must be prepared. It was to a ball of this character, that I was invited, and both the play and the ball took place within the Fort itself. I arrived at five p. m., and very soon the hall was crowded. On the platform, in front of the curtain, was seated a half-breed, a very passable violinist, who played a few military marches, followed by different national anthems, and ended with the *Marseillaise*, amid the hearty applause of all present. The curtain rose, and then began the representation of a rustic scene composed for the occasion, and entitled "Hard Times." It would take up too much space and time to give an analysis of the play ; suffice it to say that it lasted three hours, the different characters were well sustained throughout, and the hall resounded with merited applause from the spectators. The play ended, a bountiful supper was disposed of, and the play-room cleared for the dance. Here the white guests danced by themselves, and after the usual fashion, while the half-breeds, who formed the largest part of the assembly, retired to another apartment, and organized a dance of their own, and one more suited to their tastes and habits.

After viewing the whites for a length of time, I went to see how the half-breeds "trip the light fantastic." There I found four or five couples engaged in what is known as a " Red River Jig," dancing to an interminable tune played by a most wretched player, and the rest of the company seated on the floor, the men on one side of the room and the women on the other. The music never stopped, and the dancing never ceased to allow a change of sets ; but when the player got tired, he passed the violin to another, who struck up the same tune, and when a dancer got tired, he signed to another to take his place ; and thus the dance went on.

The following morning, I set out for St. Albert; a colony situated eight miles north of Edmonton, on the banks of Sturgeon Creek and the eastern shore of Big Lake. In approaching St. Albert, the Bishop's palace, the cathedral, and the orphans' home, under the superintendence of the nuns, first meet the traveller's eye. These three buildings are situated on a hill, whence the eye can behold a wide and extensive prospect. Bishop Grandin, the Roman Catholic Bishop of Saskatchewan, founded this colony by the union of some Indian and half-breed families, the latter coming from the Province of Manitoba. The above mentioned buildings are wooden structures, but they surpass in elegance all the best buildings in the North-West.

The colony of St. Albert now has a population of about 800, consisting chiefly of half-breeds and whites; the half-breeds being Franco-Indians, and the most of the whites French-Canadians.

After spending three days there, I resolved to return to Fort Saskatchewan by way of Lamoureux settlement, on Sturgeon Creek, which I had not visited for a long time. I had to travel on foot a distance of twenty-five miles, but the road had been rendered smooth by the numerous sleds which were circulating daily between Lamoureux mill and the other settlements. There was a good deal of snow, which the frequent wind-storms had driven into great heaps in some places, leaving the ground almost bare in other places.

I set out at ten a. m., and although it was in February, the day was warm. About two p.m. I arrived at Lamoureux mill, and called upon some friends with whom I took tea, and to whom I announced my approaching departure for Europe. They pressed me very kindly to stay the night with them, but it being then just sundown, and having only eight miles to walk, I thought I could easily reach Fort Saskatchewan before bed time. Bid-

ding my friends good-bye, I started ; but on leaving the
settlement, three roads lay before me; the one to the
right was the one by which I had come; the second appeared to me to lead to Edmonton, and I therefore took
the third. I would say here that it frequently happens
in the North-West, that the storms completely cover the
track, so that the first traveller after every storm is
obliged to make a road, and the track made by his sled is
invariably followed by other travellers. From this the
the reader can understand why I was puzzled which road
to take, as the road had by the above means changed its
position.

As I advanced, the road led towards Sturgeon Creek.
This could not be right since Fort Saskatchewan is four
miles above the mouth of that stream, and a little further
on, I saw that I was on the road leading to Victoria, a
settlement which is situated about sixty miles below Fort
Saskatchewan. Night had come, and the wind was
blowing violently from the north-west. What was I to
do ? The wisest course would have been to retrace my
steps and take the other road, or to accept the hospitality
of my friends. But instead of doing either, I foolishly
turned to the right across the prairie, thinking I would
soon reach the road leading to Fort Saskatchewan. But
scarcely had I taken this direction, when dense clouds,
driven by the wind, enveloped me on every side. Soon
after the snow, came in a furious storm, and the darkness
was such that I could not see two paces before me.
Sometimes I plunged into banks of snow from which I

could with difficulty extricate myself; at other times, I
stumbled into the hollows between the drifts, and although
the wind was icy cold, I perspired most freely. I should
have buried myself in a snowbank, where I could have
calmly waited the end of the story, had I not met with a
hay-stack which led me to believe I was near some habitation. In vain I stopped from time to time to take
breath, and to try to pierce the darkness; no sound save
the voice of the storm reached my ear. Completely lost,
I must have crossed the Fort Saskatchewan road by this
time, for three hours had passed since I left the road leading to Victoria. Fatigue and cold now began to overcome
me; I had only one course to pursue: I must walk as
long as my strength permitted. In order to avoid the
banks of snow as much as possible, I took a stick in
each hand, and with these felt my way. Towards midnight the clouds disappeared, and the full moon appeared
in all its splendour; and I found myself on the edge
of a forest entirely unknown to me. Remembering that
I had some matches, I gathered some dry wood with
the intention of making a good fire. But what was my
disappointment when I found that the matches had been
moistened by perspiration and would not ignite. There
was no help for it; I must continue my journey or perish.
First of all I had to discover the proper direction to take.
In the open plain the stars would have guided me, but
the wood was so dense I could not see them. However,
the trees which in these northern regions have much
thicker bark on the north side than on the south,

answered my purpose. By examining them from time to time, I knew that I was going in the proper direction.

Having got cold while endeavouring to light a fire, I now began to run in order to warm myself, and continued to run until my strength failing me, I sat down with my back against a tree. Sitting there, I began seriously, but calmly, to reflect upon my situation. At first, I thought I had done everything in my power to save my life, and it only remained for me to die ; but a slight rest gave me courage, and I concluded it would never do for one so young and vigorous to yield thus to despondency. The remembrance of other travellers too, who had struggled through circumstances quite as difficult, made me somewhat ashamed of my first thought, and taking fresh hope from their example, I set out again, determined to proceed as long as my tired legs would carry me. Very soon my efforts were rewarded by the glad sight of fresh dog tracks in the snow ; for I knew that if dogs were in the vicinity, their masters were not far off. Following the tracks, I was guided to a road with which I was not acquainted. Where was I then ? The surroundings were so entirely new to me, that I concluded in my aimless tramp, I must have wandered farther and farther from the point I was striving to reach. But before me was a road at all events ; and this I followed, in hopes of soon meeting some one who could tell me where I was, and give me food and shelter.

It was about an hour after sunrise, when from the summit of a hill, I saw two houses in the distance. "This

9

time," said I to myself, "I am wandering in my mind." (For I remembered having heard of travellers who, quite famished with hunger, took their wants for realities, and thought they saw in the distance, tables laden with the dishes which their appetite craved.) The houses I saw were not illusion however; for as I advanced, I recognised the dwelling of one of my countrymen, Mr. S., situated on the road between Edmonton and Fort Saskatchewan. I then discovered that the road I was travelling on was the one leading from Lamoureux settlement, and which joins the Edmondton and Fort Saskatchewan road, a little distance from where I then was.

Walking across the prairie to my friend's house I found the door locked; but thinking he could not be far off, I shouted for him with all my might, and I soon saw him coming from the stable, doubtlessly wondering who his early morning visitor could be. He was a long time in recognising me; for with my haggard appearance, sunken eyes, and tattered clothes, I looked more like a madman than a rational being. "What do you want, M.D." said he at last. "To go in and refresh myself," said I. With that he took his key and opened the door, and entering, he set before me a plentiful repast, which I devoured in silence. Having finished, I said to him: "My dear T., lend me a hand; I very much fear my feet are frozen." "Your feet frozen?" exclaimed he, "how?" "I have passed the night in the woods," said I, "but my story is too long to tell you now; make haste, and take off my moccassins." "Good heavens!" said he, on taking off my stockings, " your feet are indeed frozen, and very badly too." He immediately ran for a bucket of cold water, into which he put some snow, and then plunged my feet into it. But it was too late : this precaution should have been taken before entering the house. Nevertheless, I was so overcome with fatigue that I scarcely felt the excruciating pain which follows the thawing of a limb. With the help of my friend, I got into bed, where I remained the greater part of the day, and, in the evening, his neighbour, T. L., carried me in his sleigh to Fort· Saskatchewan, where for three months, I received the utmost care and attention from Dr. H. of the Mounted Police.

The news of my accident spread rapidly through the settlement, and some of the people, in order to get an idea of the distance I had traversed, tried to follow my tracks, mounted on stout horses ; but they met with such tremendous banks of snow, that they were forced to abandon their enterprise.

CHAPTER XV.

THE frost had rendered my feet in such a state that I was unable to walk for two months, and it was only towards the middle of May that I could think of taking my departure.

To get to Winnipeg, which was the nearest point where I could take the railroad, I had the choice of one of two ways; by waggon or by steamboat. The former is the most economical, but as my feet were not yet entirely healed, and I wished to see the country along the Saskatchewan, I chose the latter. The boats which ply between Winnipeg are three in number, each having its separate route to traverse. The *Lily*, which runs between Edmonton and Prince Albert, the *Northcote*, between Prince Albert and Grand Rapids, and the *Colville* (which traverses Lake Winnipeg), between Grand Rapids and Stone Fort, on Red River.

This year (1880) was the first in which the Hudson Bay Company consented to carry passengers, the fare being eighty dollars from Edmonton to Stone Fort; that is cabin passage; steerage passage being only twenty-five dollars; and in addition to the fare we had to pay fifty cents for every meal we took on board. Besides this, if for any cause the boat cannot proceed, the Company does not engage to carry the passengers by any other means to their destination.

The *Lily* had been at Edmonton all winter. She is built of steel, and is sufficiently broad and flat bottomed to sail in shallow water. In the preceding autumn, while on her way to Prince Albert, she sank near Vermilion Creek, and the passengers, among whom was the Lieut.-Governor of the North-West, had to reach Battleford in a row-boat. As for the *Lily*, which they succeeded in raising in three days, she returned to Edmonton.

In consequence of the melting of the snow in the mountains, the River began to rise about the 1st of June; but there was not enough to warrant the launching of the *Lily* until the 12th. The two following days were employed in loading with furs, and on the 15th, in the afternoon, the *Lily*, leaving Edmonton, arrived at Fort Saskatchewan at four o'clock. My preparations were completed and I went on board at once, and secured a cabin passage from there to Stone Fort. Many of the settlers came to express their regrets at my departure; all the more sincere because of the country being so thinly populated.

It was half-past five when we set out; the evening was beautiful, the boat descended the stream with wonderful speed and everything gave promise of a rapid and prosperous voyage. The cabin passengers were few; there being only two ladies of St. Albert, who were going to Montreal, and myself. The cabins on all the Saskatchewan steamers are very small, and not very comfortable when fully occupied; but happily I had one all to myself, and thus I made myself quite cosy. As for the crew it was a very Babel; for all the languages known in the North-West were spoken by them. There were both French and English Canadians, half-breeds, Indians, and even Australians. But how the latter ever reached as far as Edmonton is a mystery to me. Captain Smith, was a man of phlegmatic temperament, and well suited to manage a crew, the half of whom did not understand him, and knew absolutely nothing about the duties required of them.

Night overtook us near Vermilion Creek, and here we anchored for the night. On retiring I left my cabin door partly open to afford ventilation, for it was very warm; but I soon paid dearly for this imprudent act, for I was assailed by a swarm of mosquitoes which tortured me the whole night.

At daybreak the *Lily* resumed her voyage, and at eleven a. m. touched at Victoria to take in fuel and the Hudson Bay Company's furs. Upon the banks here were scattered pell-mell the half-breeds and Indians of Victoria, all anxious to get a view of the "fire-boat," (steamboat). All at once I saw an old friend approaching. I had met him first at Edmonton in 1874, but he left two years afterwards, and, having lost sight of him, I thought he must have said good bye to the North-West. I went to meet him, and was very much surprised to learn that he had just settled at Victoria, where he intended to devote his time to farming on a large scale.

"I am really surprised," said I to him, "that you who had such a great antipathy to the half-breeds can content yourself to live among them. Do you not think that Edmonton would be more advantageous than Victoria." "True," said he, "I would be better off at Edmonton, but I have chosen Victoria for my abode in order to induce the colonists passing this way to settle here; for if the whites do not come in and take the place of these degenerate half-breeds, in fifty years the map of the North-West will be sprinkled with black dots, representing, not the colour of the residents, but the absence of all progress in those localities. "Look," added he, "the half of those people you see on the bank have eaten nothing for two days, and this morning my house was besieged by a lot of them begging for a morsel of bread. Is it not shameful, in a fertile country where the land costs nothing? The half-breeds must be absorbed by the whites or leave the place; there is no other alternative."

It was now time for me to return to the boat, for they were beginning to withdraw the footbridge. So I bade my friend good-bye and departed, pondering on his words about the half-breeds. I had previously considered this question, and I arrived at the same conclusion; but I did not venture to express my opinions openly.

At night fall we anchored forty miles east of Victoria,

and taught by recent experience, I kept my cabin hermet-
ically closed, preferring a suffocating heat to the bites of
the mosquitoes.

About ten o'clock the next morning, we stopped a few
miles above Fort Pitt to take on board the engine of a tug
belonging to the government. Having two hours at my
disposal I went ashore to examine the neighbourhood.
The soil here is more sandy than at Victoria and Edmonton, and therefore vegetation is earlier. The landscape is
also different; for while the region around Edmonton and
Victoria is slightly undulating, that around Fort Pitt is
quite hilly.

That afternoon we arrived at Fort Pitt, and, hearing
from the captain that we were going to stop three hours,
I resolved to consecrate that time in visiting that locality.

This colony is situated on the left bank of the Saskatchewan, in a plain gradually rising in amphitheatre
to a certain height, whence a wide prospect presents
itself to view. Around the Fort, which is enclosed by a
feeble stockade, one sees some small rustic houses, inhab-
itated by half-breeds, some Indian wigwams whose owners
have come to exchange furs for goods, and a small garden
adjoining the stockade of the Fort, which is cultivated by
the employees of the Company.

On landing, I went towards one of the small houses, at
the entrance of which, a half-breed was seated, content-
edly smoking his pipe. This fellow was not wanting in
politeness, for seeing my approach, he arose, and taking
off a dirty hat which he must have inherited from his

ancestors, he invited me to enter. In a single apartment, some twelve feet either way, which served as parlour, dining-room, kitchen and bedroom, five children, scantily dressed in rags, were rolling on the floor, while the mother was swinging a sixth in a hammock. No chairs were to be seen, the half-breed being contented to sit on the floor, but an empty box was produced for my accommodation. Finding my entertainer very loquacious, I resolved to get from him all the information possible. " Now that the buffaloes have almost disappeared," said I to him, " would it not be better for you to renounce this wandering life and cultivate the soil ? What do you do here ? I do not see even a garden near your house." " I am in the service of the Hudson Bay Company," he replied ; " but I would cultivate the soil, if I had what is necessary ; cattle, agricultural implements, and above all, enough provisions for a year. Let the government come to the aid of the half-breeds, and they will soon become farmers." " The government will take good care not to do so," said I. "and for very good reasons. If the half-breeds are still in poverty, they have only themselves to blame ; for with the fur trade, it would have been easy to realize great profits. You are in a more favourable position than many of the colonists ; for you have horses at least, while they have only their hands with which to gain a livelihood. Bear this in mind, that, before very long, this country will undergo a complete transformation, and if, in the meantime, you have not made yourselves independent, you will be obliged to retire into the wild regions, or become the servants of

the whites." Saying this, I started to visit the neighbourhood, followed by the half-breed.

" You Frenchmen from France," said he, as he accompanied me to the boat, " you always give us good advice
Your missionaries are constantly telling us to plough and
sow, and educate ourselves, if we do not want to be sup-
planted by the whites—to take possession of the best
lands and public offices, etc. But our opinion is that with
a gun and a horse, we have all that we require. We are
wanting in foresight and energy, but the half-breed is so
constituted. I thank you for your visit and advice, however, and wish you a safe and prosperous journey."

From Fort Pitt to Battleford, the current becomes less
swift, and sand banks are encountered, upon which boats,
guided even by experienced pilots, are sometimes stranded,
These sand-banks, invisible when the water is muddy,
occasion no other inconvenience than that of unloading the
the stranded boats in order to get them afloat again. To
avoid this, the *Lily*, on leaving Fort Pitt, slackened her speed.
That day, we felt only some slight shocks ; but the next
morning, we encountered so many sand-banks, we could
not clear them all, and about eight o'clock the *Lily* suddenly came to a stop. After trying in vain to back off,
we succeeded in getting her afloat by means of the capstan and spars which were placed in the water and worked
with pulleys, and two hours later, we came to anchor on
the right bank of the river, one mile above Battleford.

Learning that we would not set out again till the next
day, I directed my steps towards the town, which I had

never seen. While approaching a house where I hoped to get information concerning the place, I suddenly heard myself called by name, and turning I beheld a constable of the North-West Mounted Police, who was in the campaign of 1874 with me, and from him I gathered all the information I required.   A little farther on, lay the town in a valley of about three-quarters of a mile in length.   Battle River divides it into two parts by emptying itself into the Saskatchewan River. The part on the left bank contains the residence of the Lieutenant-Governor, the fort of the Mounted Police, and a few scattered houses ; but on the right bank, is the greatest part of the town, where one notices the Roman Catholic Church and the printing office of the *Saskatchewan Herald,* the only newspaper in that country.

Battleford is the Capital of the North-West Territories and although its founding dates only from 1876, it possesses a population of about eight hundred inhabitants, most of them half-breeds and whites.   Being situated at the junction of the Saskatchewan and Battle River, and on the line of the Canadian Pacific Railway, this town will, before long, become one of the greatest commercial centres of the North-West.

At night-fall I returned to the *Lily,* on board of which a number of the inhabitants of the town were congregated, bidding farewell to two of their fellow-townsmen who were going; one, Mr. M., across the Atlantic, for the benefit of his health, and the other, Mr. R., only as far as

Winnipeg. Destined to travel together, we were not long
in forming an acquaintance.

At day-break, we resumed our voyage, hoping to arrive
early at Carleton; but we had not made allowance for a
contrary wind which blew with great violence during the
whole of the day. We soon arrived at the elbow where
the river turns towards the north in a direction parallel
to the South Saskatchewan, from which it is separated
by a distance of only fifteen miles, and with it, forms, from
the elbow to the confluence, a peninsula of about ninety
miles in length. Judging only from the soil of this peninsula, one is inclined to believe that it has been formed by
successive alluvial deposits from the rivers.

The sun was setting when we came in view of Carleton.
The *Lily* put in to the right bank, opposite the Hudson
Bay Co.'s Fort, amid the cries of the Indians and half-
breeds congregated on the shore. Here we were greatly
disappointed in hearing from Mr. Clarke, the director of
the Fort, that the steamer *Northcote* would probably not
arrive before the 20th of July. We could have reached
Winnipeg by means of vehicles, but we decided to proceed as far as Prince Albert by the *Lily* where we would
come to a definite conclusion.

The next day, Sunday, the 20th of June, hearing that
the boat would not leave before one o'clock in the afternoon, I went on shore to visit Carleton once more. This
colony has made but little progress since 1874; the only
change I noticed was a new house built by Mr. Clark.

That same day, at five o'clock in the evening, we arrived

at Prince Albert, and anchored near the warehouse of the Hudson Bay Co. We at once held a consultation as to the best course to pursue in consequence of the delay of the *Northcote.* Some were in favour of purchasing horses and carriages to continue the journey; others thought it more prudent to await the arrival of the steamer. Four of us, however, Messrs. R. and M., whom the reader already knows, Mr. G., from Edmonton, and I, resolved to purchase a skiff in which to descend as far as Grand Rapids. This adventurous voyage, according to the pilot of the *Lily,* was to be very agreeable and could be accomplished in about ten days. Not to lose any time Mr. ●. and myself went in search of a skiff. We examined the canoes and skiffs in the vicinity, but none of them being large and strong enough to carry ourselves and our luggage,—we therefore returned to the *Lily* and acquainted our companions with the result of our proceedings.

As we were discussing what was best to do next, an Anglo-Indian half-breed came up, saying that he could construct, in a very short time, a boat capable of carrying six persons: he had been one of an expedition under Sir John Franklin to the Polar Sea.

"How long will it take you to build such a boat?" said Mr. R. "Five days at the most," answered the half-breed. "What price do you ask?" "Forty dollars, and you furnish the material." Fearing my companions would take his offer I interposed, remarking that it was much too dear, and the more so as we were not absolutely obliged to have the boat built. "If you will build the skiff for twenty dollars," said I to him, " we will give you that amount, but no more."

My abrupt interference probably wounded the self-importance of the half-breed, for he went away without making a reply. But I understood those people too well to be imposed upon by any of them. I knew he would return, which in a short time he did, excusing himself for having gone away without replying to my proposition, and offering to construct the boat for twenty-two dollars if we would furnish the material. This we agreed to, and the next day he set to work.

Mr. R. had the happy idea of taking a tent, and offered to share it with me ; and I willingly accepted, not caring to take lodgings in any of the hotels of Prince Albert.

The Prince Albert settlement is one of the oldest and most important colonies of the North-West. It begins ten miles below Carleton and extends as far as the confluence of the two branches of the Saskatchewan. There are at present three rising towns in different localities of the settlement, the principal of which is Goshen, a landing place for steamers and having some stores, a saw-mill and a grist-mill, both driven by steam.

Prince Albert possesses three churches and several schools. The inhabitants, who are widely scattered and, whose number is unknown, cultivate cereals with success, the region being extremely fertile.

CHAPTER XVI.

Departure from Prince Albert—Cole Rapids—Fort à la Corne—A Lesson on
Geography—Loss of a Part of Our Provisions—Bear Hunting—Birch Is-
lands—Mosquito Point—Cumberland—Trunks of Trees Encumbering the
Banks of the River—Our Arrival at Pas Mission.

ON Friday, the 25th of June, the skiff was finished,
and our departure was fixed for the next day.
We had been assured that, at that season of the year, it
was impossible to procure provisions at any of the Forts
on our route; hence, we took with us sufficient supplies
to last twelve days; and to be prepared for every contin-
gency, we also took an extra 100 pounds of flour; the
sequel will show that this was necessary precaution. I
shall never forget the kindness we received at the hands
of the Hudson Bay officers, for not only did they give
us all necessary information, but they directed a half-
breed to pilot us all the way to Grand Rapids. This
guide, as will be seen, was far from meriting our confidence.

We passed the night of the 26th under Mr. R's tent, and
at two o'clock the next morning I awoke my companions;
we prepared breakfast in the open air, and started at five
a.m. A short time after, we landed at the Hudson Bay
Company's Fort, where we had appointed to meet our
guide. He had not yet arrived, and I made the remark that

the boat was heavily laden enough without him, and that, if it was absolutely necessary, we could find a guide at any of the Forts situated on our route. My companions nevertheless insisted on waiting for the half-breed, but it was near six o'clock, and he had not yet appeared. . We were speculating as to what could be the cause for his delay, when I remembered that he crossed the evening before with our boat, and I remarked to my companions that he had doubtless done this to try her strength, and not being satisfied with it, he would not come. This conclusion settled the matter, and we set out immediately. Mr. R., being the oldest, took the helm, Mr. G. and myself the oars, and Mr. M. although ill, acted as pilot. The town of Goshen soon disappeared behind us, and in three hours we expected to reach Cole Rapids. We soon found out that the current was swift enough to impart sufficient speed to our boat; so Mr. G. and F. agreed to row in turns, except in the rapids, where we could not go too fast. For three hours we had sailed along without seeing any sign of these famous rapids, so very dangerous, according to the accounts of the inhabitants of Prince Albert, who had advised us to have our boat conveyed by waggon as far as the junction (twenty miles off), and to embark there.

From time to time we stopped to listen to the least noise that might indicate the proximity of the rapids, at last Mr. M. called out: "Look here! if we waste our time in listening to imaginary noises, we shall never see Grand Rapids. I doubt very much whether the half-breeds and Indians of the North-West know what a rapid

is." Messrs. R. and G. seemed to share the opinion of Mr.
M., but I was of quite a different opinion, remembering
that a steamer, belonging to the Hudson's Bay Company,
had foundered while ascending a rapid.

Full of hope, my companions fancied themselves already
near the end of their journey, when, just as we were approaching a tongue of land which projected into the middle of the river, a rumbling noise like the roar of a cataract
interrupted their merry conversation. After turning the
point, we saw about a mile head of us, a hill which appeared to connect the two banks of the river, and in
which the waters seemed to lose themselves. The farther
we advanced, the more rapid the stream became. Soon
not far from the hill, the foaming crests of the waves appeared, which were doubtless the beginning of the rapids.
" What shall we do ? " said Mr. R., " do you think we
should land in order to examine the rapids before running
them." " Yes, let us land," said Mr. G. and I together, " we
must not be imprudent." "What!" exclaimed Mr. M., " one
would think you had never seen a rapid." Notwithstanding his protestation, we persisted in rowing towards the left
bank ; but instead of landing, we found ourselves on the
brink of the rapid, and descending stern foremost. It
was a critical moment ! With a few vigorous strokes of
the paddle, Mr. R. turned the boat, and a moment later,
we were in the midst of the rapids with the waves boiling and surging on every side. Once a huge wave, rising
several feet above the level of the boat, came dashing
towards us and I thought we would surely be swamped,

10

But the boat arose as the wave approached, and we escaped with only a plentiful shower—both Mr. J. and myself did our best to assist Mr. R. in command of the boat, and avoiding the rocks against which the waves dashed with fury, then recoiled upon themselves and turned abruptly to the right.

Having passed this rock, we were out of danger, and Mr. M., who had affected to despise the rapids of the North-West, was compelled to admit that this one was sufficiently dangerous to satisfy his love of adventures.

Before reaching the junction, we had still five rapids to run, and two of them proved more dangerous than that we had just run. But at two o'clock we had safely passed them all, and landed at a grove to dine.

The Cole Rapids extend a distance of about ten miles, and between two consecutive rapids there is on an average a distance of one mile. At the bottom of each rapid, as we have seen from the first, there is a hill which serves as a signal of approaching danger. The steamboats ascend these rapids by means of the capstan and cables fastened to trees along the banks. This explains why it takes four days for them to go from the junction to Prince Albert, although they descend them with amazing rapidity.

I would advise all travellers who wish to examine that natural phenomenon, to follow our example by taking a row boat as the steamers descend too swiftly to permit one to observe it closely.

At half past two, we resumed our journey, and soon

reached the junction of the two branches of the Saskatchewan, where there are a few houses, among which, one
discovers the one Captain Butler had built during his
journey to the northern regions. The reason he built
that house was that he thought that the Canadian Pacific
Railroad would cross the Saskatchewan at that place ;
and his belief has been shared by a great number of colonists who have settled there.

The two branches of the Saskatchewan form a large
river, and its swift current, together with the strokes of
the oars, sent us along with great velocity.

About five o'clock that evening, we saw before us on
the right bank of the river, a volume of smoke ascending
from a wood. We steered for it, thinking it was Fort à
la Corne. Fastening our boat to a tree, we ascended the
bank, entered the wood and soon came to a cabin, which
indicated the presence of Indians and half-breeds. Near
the cabin was an inclosure, in the centre of which was a
fire from which issued the smoke we had seen ; and outside of which stood a number of cattle, greatly tormented
by the mosquitoes. Aroused by their dogs, the inhabitants came out, and seemed not a little terrified by our
presence. We spoke to them in English, French, and
Cree, but without avail, and we were compelled to return
to our boat, without obtaining any information.

A little further on, we came in view of a group of
houses, on the left bank which led us to believe that we
had already passed Fort à la Corne, which, according to
the instructions we had received at Prince Albert, was

situated on the right bank of the river, and was the first settlement we would meet after leaving the junction. But very soon the Fort which a projecting point had prevented us from seeing, came into view, and we saw before us a stockade built of hewn timber, within which was the Fort, the whole surrounded by woods. It was seven o'clock when we landed, and we proceeded at once to the house of Mr. Goodfellow, director of the Fort, who offered to entertain us. He is a man about fifty years of age, endowed with a wonderful memory, and thoroughly versed in the geography of the Saskatchewan. After the experience of the day, we thought it would be well to take a guide the rest of the distance, and inquired of Mr. Goodfellow if he knew one whom he could recommend.

"A guide," said he, "you can easily do without one; for, although you are unacquainted with the river, I will give you all the information necessary to carry you safely through."

After a moment of reflection, he continued : " By rowing well, you can reach Grand Rapids in five days. Tomorrow, by setting out early and travelling all day, you will reach Birch Islands, where it will be hard for you to find a favourable place for camping, because, at present, the river overflows the banks. Below Birch Islands you will find the Tobin Rapids which you will easily run. Farther down, on the left bank, you will see Paskatinow Hill where you can take dinner. On leaving this place always keep along the right bank; for a few miles farther, at Mosquito Point, the river divides into two principal branches, of which the one on the left would take you into the Sturgeon River, and from there into Lake Cumberland where you would inevitably lose yourselves. In one day, by rowing vigorously, you will reach a cabin on the left bank three or four miles from Lake Cumberland, where you can pass the night, since it is uninhabited and the doors are always open. Then, one day will take you to Pas Mission where the employees of the Hudson Bay Company will esteem it a pleasure to give you more exact information. After leaving Pas Mission in one day you will reach the Indian Colony at the entrance of Cedar Lake. Between Pas Mission and this lake the river, in some places, divides into several branches. Always take the first to the right, for the others lead into vast swamps, among aquatic plants, out of which it is difficult to extricate one's self. Below the Indian Colony you will enter Cedar Lake and coast along its left shore as far as the entrance of a large bay, whence, if the atmosphere is clear, you will see Rabbit Point, towards the extremity of which you will steer. On turning this point you will re-enter the bed of the river, and in a few hours you will be at Grand Rapids."

Just as Mr. Goodfellow ended speaking a half-breed woman announced that supper was served.

" I am really sorry, gentlemen," said the Director, " that I can offer you nothing but dry meat. The Fort has never been so scantily provided with provisions. I hope that the director of Fort Cumberland whom I expect every moment, will bring me some supplies, otherwise I shall not know what to do until the *Northcote* arrives."

We thought it our duty to refuse this generous invitation, and returned to the boat, intending to invite the director to supper; but a disagreeable surprise awaited us there, the bread, the meat, and part of the butter had disappeared. Mr. M., who could never control his temper, began to storm against the inhabitants of Fort à la Corne, whom he denounced as thieves. I hesitated to coincide with his opinion, not thinking the Indians and half-breeds capable of committing such an audacious theft, and I was right; for beside the boat, on the bank, I saw some dogs' tracks which I showed to my companions, and the dogs proved to be the real thieves. On making examination, we had yet remaining some potatoes, ten pounds of butter, and the hundred pound sack of flour. Mr. M. declared that he was tired of this pleasure voyage, and that he would go no farther. We made him understand, not without difficulty, that sick as he was, and unable to procure the necessaries of life, it was better for him to come with us, since, in a few days, we would reach Grand Rapids. He ended by embracing our opinion, and we pitched our tent for the night.

The next day, at three o'clock in the morning, we resumed our journey, resolved to reach Birch Islands before night. As on the preceding day, Mr. R. took the helm, Mr. G. and I. the oars, while Mr. M. indicated the direction to follow. The weather was splendid, and the skiff shot forward rapidly; hence our good humour, which had been disturbed by the loss of our provisions, returned at the thought that we were soon going to meet the director of Fort Cumberland, from whom we could buy supplies.

Mr. M., who was on the look out, perceived ahead of us four canoes which were ascending the current. At first sight, we thought it was the director of Fort Cumberland but we soon discovered, to our great disappointment, that they were Indians on their way to Fort à la Corne with canoes laden with various kinds of furs which they were going to exchange for merchandise. We landed, and Mr. M. asked them in Cree, if they had any meat for sale. Poor wretches! they were quite surprised at such a question ; for they had eaten nothing for two days. We gave them a few pounds of flour, and in return they left us a beaver skin.

About nine o'clock, we reached Pinnacle Bend, where there are three consecutive rapids which we ran without difficulty, as they for length and danger cannot be compared to Cole Rapids.

From Fort à la Corne, the banks of the river become gradually lower until at Birch Islands they are submerged and accordingly we landed at the foot of these rapids, fearing that farther on we should not find so convenient a place to dine. We hoped to pass Birch Islands that day but we had not taken into account a violent wind which arose in the afternoon, and which retarded the progress of the boat. This delay disappointed us, Mr. M. who could not accustom himself to our low diet, was especially affected by it.

About five o'clock in the afternoon, we noticed that the farther we advanced, the wider the river became and its banks were covered with birch wood. This was an evident proof that we were not far from Birch Islands.

"My friends," said Mr. M., "if we are without meat this evening, it will be our own fault. Very probably, we shall encounter some bears crossing the river. These encounters are very frequent, if we can believe the travellers who have visited this part of the country. Prepare yourselves for a hunt."

Mr. M. was right, for we soon saw, about a mile ahead of us, a black object, crossing the river, which proved to be a bear. Mr. R. and I. undertook the management of the boat, while Mr. G. armed with an axe, placed himself in the prow, to knock the animal in the head, as soon as he should get within reach.

"Under present circumstances," said Mr. M., "a bear-steak is not to be despised. As it would take some time to skin the animal and prepare the meat, I propose that we go no farther for to-day." "Not so fast Mr. M." answered I, "don't sell the skin of the bear before killing him." At the same instant, the prow of the boat struck the animal. Mr. G. with great "sans-froid," dealt him two blows with the axe upon the head; but the bear, although a little stunned, continued to swim towards the shore. Mr. G. had neglected to strike with the edge. He was preparing to do so, when the axe, slipping from his hands, fell into the water. "Strike him with the oars" exclaimed Mr. M. when he saw the bear was getting away from us.

But the animal was already too far. Mr. R then handed him his gun, which, loaded with shot, produced no effect. After reaching the shore the bear looked at us for a moment and then disappeared in the forest.

" Well," said I to Mr. M., " do you find the bear-steak palatable ? " Mr. M., who did not relish the jest, dwelt greatly upon our situation which was becoming more and more critical, for we had scarcely any provisions and no axe to cut wood. But he was reassured a little by the fact that Mr. R. had a revolver, with which we probably could procure some game.

About sunset, we arrived at Birch Islands, which extend a distance of about ten miles. As their name indicates, they are covered with birch trees, with the bark of which the Indians construct their canoes. We sailed along these islands, following the right shore ; and we were overtaken by night before reaching the lower extremity. These islands being almost entirely submerged, it was difficult to find a dry spot to camp. For a while we thought of letting the boat drift, but such a course would have been very imprudent, as the Tobin Rapids were a short distance below. After a great deal of searching, we found at last a spot somewhat dry which we rendered comfortable by means of branches. We slept very little that night, being nearly devoured by the mosquitoes which, in this region, are almost equal to young grasshoppers in size.

At three o'clock next morning, we put off, and soon reached the lower extremity of the islands, from whence

the roar of the rapids is distinctly heard. We easily ran
these, and landed at the foot of them, to take breakfast.
About ten o'clock we arrived in sight of Mosquito Point,
in the neighbourhood of which there are some sand-banks.
The river, which is here very wide, divides into two
branches. We took the one to the right, according to the
directions of Mr. Goodfellow, and on turning Mosquito
Point, we were assailed by a very strong wind, which,
blowing against the current, raised formidable waves.
We advanced very slowly, and therefore despaired of
reaching Cumberland the same evening.

The branch of the river, which we had entered, was becoming more and more narrow, and my travelling companions (especially Mr. R.) were of the opinion that we
had taken the wrong route, and it would be necessary for
us to retrace our steps. I interfered in order to express
an opinion altogether different.

" We are," said I, " only following the directions given
us. If we are not in the right way, we have been de-
ceived, which is a very improbable supposition, since the
information obtained up to the present moment, although
emanating from different sources, agrees in every point."
" I am far from thinking" replied Mr. R., " that Mr. Goodfellow and the inhabitants of Prince Albert wanted to de-
ceive us ; but I notice that the river is gradually getting
narrower, and is taking us to the south, instead of towards the east as the map indicates." " You forget," said
I " that we are just rounding Mosquito Point, and, in that
case I would not be at all surprised, even if we turned to-

wards the south. It is impossible to mark on the map all the windings of a river."

My arguments were not able to convince them. For a long time, I opposed every thought of turning back ; but, obliged to yield to the opinion of the majority, I insisted on waiting half an hour, promising that if, at the end of that time, nothing indicated that we were on the right way, I would concur in their opinion. They regretfully granted me that request ; but they had no reason to repent of it, for soon we perceived on the right of the river, some piles of wood which the Hudson Bay Company had prepared for the steamboats. We were therefore on the right way. By retracing our steps, we would have taken, at Mosquito Point, the branch to the left which would have led us into Sturgeon River which we had been particularly cautioned to avoid.

The day was drawing to a close, and we had not yet perceived the cabin of which Mr. Goodfellow had spoken of. It was strange ; for we had travelled rapidly the whole day, and, according to the map we had with us, the distance from Fort à la Corne to Birch Islands is equal or about equal to that between these islands and the cabin. Mr. M. and G. expressed the opinion that we had already passed it. As for Mr. R., he still adhered to the idea that we were astray, and that we would be obliged to go back. He therefore was not a little surprised next day, after an hour's rowing, to see on the left bank of the river a cabin built of hewn logs. This structure is used to receive the supplies brought by the *North-*

cote, and intended for Fort Cumberland situated on the lake of that name. This Hudson Bay Company's Fort is connected with the cabin above mentioned by a small stream hardly deep enough to carry small boats.

Mr. R. proposed that we should row up to Fort Cumberland and lay in another supply of provisions ; but we thought it better to continue our journey, and try to reach Pas Mission that evening.

From Cumberland to Pas Mission, the banks of the river were completely submerged, and crowded with floating trunks of trees, having the form of rafts. It was on these logs that we prepared and took our meals, and this is how these rafts are formed. At the time of high water, in the part of the river, lying between Prince Albert and the Rocky Mountains, great land slips occur on the steep banks, whose trees are uprooted, and carried away by the current. In those places where the river is on a level with the banks, it is enough that one end of the tree becomes entangled in the aquatic plants in order to stop the others, and form a kind of raft.

Night came without anything occurring to indicate the proximity of Pas Mission. Thinking that it was not prudent to camp on the rafts, we continued our journey, and towards ten o'clock, we saw some fire on the right bank of the river. We steered towards it, and found there were some Indians camping there. Mr. M. asked them how far we were from Pas Mission. They replied that we would soon be there. With the Indians " soon" may signify two days as well as two hours. Midnight arrived and no dwelling was in sight. We began to think we had passed Pas Mission, and, at all events, it was time to take some rest. So, after having landed, and fastened our boat to a tree, we went to sleep in the bottom of the boat.

At two o'clock next morning we set out again, and, at daylight, we came in sight of some houses and a large lake. Taking this lake for Cedar Lake and the houses for the Indian Colony, we started towards these dwellings in hope of buying some fish from the Indians. We found nobody within the house we entered, but the fire burning on the hearth proved to us that the owners were not far off. After waiting there for a while and being resolved to wait no longer, we were starting towards another house when we saw two Indians coming towards us. They were returning from fishing and had with them a great quantity of fish, some of which they exchanged with us for flour. We asked them if that large sheet of water was Cedar Lake.

" My white brothers are distant from it," answered the oldest of the two. " What my brothers see is not a lake but a plain which the river overflows when the water is high. My brothers see at the extremity of this the houses of Pas Mission."

After breakfast we took leave of the Indians and re-sumed our journey, and an hour later we landed on the right bank, in front of the Hudson Bay Company's fort,

CHAPTER XVII.

THE Pas Mission Settlement is one of the most popu-
lous in the North-West Territories. The inhabitants, almost all Indians and half-breeds, dwell on the
banks of the river, in cottages built upon rocks, and are
thus safe from the floods. The Hudson Bay Company's
Fort, which is the landing place of the Steamboats, is situated at the mouth of the Carrot River, which waters a
vast and fertile region, and it is my opinion that, in a
very short time, the tide of emigration will flow towards
those parts, where a Province will probably be formed
with Pas Mission for its capital.

Having landed, we followed the directions of Mr. Goodfellow, and went towards the Hudson Bay Company's
Fort, where we met its director, who gave us a hearty
welcome. Some travellers have related, and still relate,
that the officers of the Hudson Bay Company are inhos-
pitable ; but this is a sheer slander. The director of the
Fort, who frequently goes to Grand Rapids, gave us very
definite information about the part of the river we had

still to travel. He was quite surprised that we had dared to descend Cole Rapids in such a frail bark.

" You have yet to run," said he, "the most dangerous and imposing rapids, and if you are afraid of forgetting my instructions, I will write them down for you."

" It is not necessary," we replied, "give them orally."

After a moment's reflection, he continued : " From here to Cedar Lake, the banks being submerged, it will be difficult for you to camp. It is already nine o'clock ; I doubt very much whether you can reach the lake before night. Five or six miles from here, the river divides into two branches of which you will take the smaller to the right. By following the other you would also arrive at your destination, but as it is longer, you would lose time uselessly. After a pretty long course, these two branches unite again. Farther on, the river separates into several branches which unite to only separate again. Always take the first branch to the right even if it be smaller than the others which lead into immense lakes formed by the over-flowing of the river. If you travel during the night, let one of you keep watch in order to avoid going astray. As for houses, you will only meet with the Indian Settlement of Cedar Lake. If the weather be fine, you can enter the lake without danger, and coasting along the left shore, you will thus arrive at the entrance of a large bay, whence you will see Rabbit Point, which appears to be separated from the right bank, by a canal through which the current of the river flows. You will steer for this point, and after turning it, you will follow the left shore. Two or three hours afterwards, you will see that the river divides into two branches. Take the one to the left. Beware of taking the other, which would lead you into rapids where you would infallibly founder. After entering the left branch, you will hear the roaring of the "Demi-Charge" which is at the entrance of Cross Lake. Advance carefully, and when near the rapids, land on the left bank, then following a foot-path which extends along the shore, you will let the boat descend by means of two ropes attached, one to the stern, the other to the prow. Before entering Cross Lake, the river separates into three branches, forming as many rapids; but that which you will follow by keeping along the shore, is the least dangerous. You will re-embark at the foot of the "Demi-Charge," and, after crossing the lake, you will reach Little Red-Rock Rapid, which you will run without difficulty. From there you will hear the noise of the Red Rock Rapid, which you will run, keeping close to the right shore. From the foot of this last rapid, you will see, at some distance, on the left bank, the Hudson Bay Company's Fort, situated above Grand Rapids, which is the end of your journey."

The directions of the director of Pas Mission completed those of Mr. Goodfellow, who had not spoken of the rapids lying on our route.

At ten o'clock we set out again, and as the director said, we soon arrived at the point where the river forms two branches. That to the right is so small, that we thought it was not the right one. We took it, however, in order to follow the instructions received, and we did not regret it, for it proves to be the right one. Two hours later, we rejoined the left branch.

According as the distance from Pas Mission increases, the banks of the river become gradually lower. At night-fall, we wished to camp, but there was not a single tree to which we could moor the boat. Around us, lay an immense lake, streaked here and there with strips of . aquatic plants. After deliberating as to the best course to pursue, we agreed to travel all night, allowing the boat to drift; only, it was decided that, not to deviate from our instructions, we would keep watch, each in his turn. It fell to my lot to be the first on watch, and after me, came Mr. R. I had just gone to sleep, when he awakened us suddenly, exclaiming that we had entered a channel to the left, and that consequently, it was necessary to go back.

"One soon finds out when Mr. R. is on sentry." said Mr. M. For two consecutive nights, we have hardly slept. Can't we, at least, rest this one night ? "

"If I have awakened you," replied Mr. R., "it is because we have just taken a direction which we were carefully recommended to avoid."

"We have just taken !" retorted Mr. M., "say rather, I have taken. It is you who are on guard. Besides, by following the channel which, like the others, must end at Cedar Lake, we cannot help arriving there. In the meantime, talk no more about directions given or re-

11

ceived ; if the inhabitants of this country heard us, they would imagine that we don't know anything."

I was already at the oars, but after the objurgation of Mr. M., I did not think it proper to interfere, in order to return. A short while afterwards. Mr. R. awoke me, saying to me in French, "there is only three feet of water." I got up and asked him what he thought of the situation. "We have done a very foolish thing," said he, "in following the advice of Mr. M., I greatly fear we shall repent of it."

I took the oars, in order to go faster, for, according as we advanced, the current became less rapid. The depth of the water decreased in the same proportion, and soon the boat touched bottom. Notwithstanding the darkness which enveloped us, we thought we saw before us, a vast sheet of water which Mr. M. declared to be Cedar Lake.

"You see now" said he, "that by following any direction whatever, one always comes out all right. Now rest yourselves. At day break we shall steer for the Indian settlement where we will buy enough fish for the whole day. I hope to breakfast to-morrow on board the *Colville* at Grand Rapids."

At daybreak, I got up first, to see this lake so extolled by Mr. M. But what was my disappointment, when, instead of a lake, I beheld vast marshes covered at intervals with aquatic plants. I awoke my comrades, who were astonished to hear this news. We held a consultation, before taking any definite action. I proposed that we

should go back, although it would be a half day's work ;
but they said that, since we were so far, we must advance, and if possible, open a way through the aquatic
plants. Obliged to yield to the opinion of the majority.
we resumed our journey rowing towards the right, hoping
to find soon the bed of the river. But according as we
advanced, I noticed that the water, muddy as it was, was
becoming gradually clearer like marshy water. From
this, I inferred that, instead of approaching the river, we
were going away from it, and I stated my fears to my
travelling companions ; but they were so excited, that
they did not cease to advance, until, stopped by the reeds,
they told me that they resigned themselves entirely to
me. As I had rowed the preceding day, and the greater
part of the night, I felt fatigued ; so, giving the oars to
the others, I took the helm, and announced that we would
turn back. My decision was received without a murmur ;
for it was the wisest course to take after so many fruitless attempts. As we were retracing our steps, I thought
I saw, at a great distance, some trunks of trees piled one
above the other. I then remembered those logs which
strew the banks of the river between Cumberland and
Pas Mission, and below this last settlement. From this,
I inferred that if they were trees, the branch of the river
that had drifted them was not far off. Nevertheless,
fearing I might be mistaken, I abstained from imparting
my reflections to my companions, but they soon made the
remark we were going to the right instead of going back,
as I had announced on taking the management of the

boat. "In ten minutes, at the latest," I exclaimed, "we shall enter the bed of the river. That surprises you, but you have the proof before your eyes."

"What proof?" said Mr. M. opening his eyes, and, looking alternately to the right and to the left, forward and backward, he declared that he did not see anything.

"Do you see those trunks of trees?" said I, "Yes, but what have they to do with the river," said he. "You shall see," said I.

Hardly had we passed these logs, when a swift current imparted a great speed to the boat. We were on a branch of the river, and seeing a thicket on the other bank, we steered towards it in order to take breakfast. The thicket was submerged, and we were obliged to prepare our meal as well as we could upon the floating tree trunks.

After breakfast which consisted of tea, bread and butter, a discussion arose between Mr. M. and R., concerning the cause of our going astray, which Mr. G. put an end to by observing that we were not yet out of danger, and that it was imprudent to lose time in useless discussions, which might be better employed in trying to reach the Indians of Cedar Lake, where we could purchase fish.

As Mr. G. observed, we were not yet at the end of our troubles. A little farther the branch of the river in which we were then divides into two others. We made the mistake of taking the left, and soon found ourselves in the midst of a rapid which carried us to a lake several leagues in circumference. We determined to coast along the shores in order to find an outlet; but, after rowing several hours without success, encountering nothing but reeds, which encircled the lake, we came to the conclusion that it was better to land somewhere to take some rest. The difficulty was to find a dry spot, and therefore I advised my friends that we should row towards the middle of the lake, whence we could have a better view. My suggestion was followed, and before long, we perceived, some miles ahead of us, a series of fir thickets. In the first grove, to the right, stood a gigantic fir, whose mid branches had been lopped off.

"Surely," said Mr. R., "he who climbed that tree, did not take such dangerous exercise merely to amuse himself. He had a serious motive for doing so."

We steered towards this grove, and it was well we did, for, half an hour later, a violent wind arose which raised the waves, and exposed us to the greatest danger until we approached the grove, which was surrounded with reeds, through which it was impossible to propel the boat. We were then sheltered from the storm, and Mr. R., Mr. G., and I, fatigued by continued labour during two days and two nights, fell asleep. Fortunately, Mr. M. kept watch for us. He soon woke us up, exclaiming that the wind was carrying us out into open water, and that we must land at any cost. After sailing for some time along the reeds we found a passage which conducted us to the grove. It was in reality a kind of island, about two miles in circumference, twelve feet high, and formed of layers of rock. This was the first time that we had camped on a dry place since leaving Fort à la Corne. So, forgetting our precarious condition, I took my blankets and lay down in the shade of a fir.

Judging by the deep marks which the waves have left on the shore, the grove which afforded us a shelter was formerly an island situated in a permanent lake, whose disappearance can be explained by the two following causes.

Lake Winnipeg and Cedar Lake have a difference of sixty feet between their levels, and are only about thirty miles distant from each other; hence the rapids which lie between them.   But, between these two lakes, the bed of the river being constantly excavated by the waters, this produces a corresponding fall in the level of Cedar Lake. Moreover, by taking account of the successive alluvial deposits from the river, one sees that a time will come when Cedar Lake will have completely disappeared.   The same causes will contribute to the disappearance of Lake Winnipeg, whose waters, escaping by the Nelson River, flow into Hudson Bay, after a descent of seven hundred and ten feet in a course of three hundred and eighty miles.

One can, therefore, affirm that the grove in which we were camped, was formerly a permanent island, situated in Cedar Lake, which extended as far as Cumberland, judging from the alluvial deposits which cover that region, and its submersion by the river during the time of the floods.   Before long, this region will very probably furnish rich pasture lands.

I had slept a few hours when I felt a hand lightly

touch my shoulder, and, on turning, I saw Mr. M., who, with a smile on his lips, informed me that Mr. R., from the top of a tree, had seen the *Northcote* ascending the river. We were, therefore, not far from being on the right road. I got up at once and advised an immediate departure. Mr. G., modifying the version of Mr. M., told me that Mr. R. had seen the smoke of the steamboat. But Mr. R., coming down from his observatory, cut short our preparations for departure by declaring that he was not sure of having seen the smoke. We therefore pitched the tent for the night and prepared enough bread for two or three days in order to start early the next morning. During the night an impetuous wind arose which exposed us to unexpected dangers. The trees, whose roots were not very deep, were violently shaken and threatened to crush us in their fall. It would therefore have been imprudent to remain under the tent, so we went out and did not return until the storm was over.

At day-break we got ready to depart. The wind was yet very high; the waves breaking with fury upon the rocks of the islands, and the sky was overcast with dark lowering clouds which were going to resolve into rain. Mr. R. and Mr. G. suggested to wait till the storm was over, but Mr. M. and I were of the opinion that it was better to face the waves than hunger. Mr. G. finally concurred with us, on condition that we should steer towards a row of islands which appeared to be about three miles distant. So Mr. R. took the helm, and we set out. As long as we were sailing amongst the high grasses which surrounded the island, the waves did not seriously annoy us, and we congratulated ourselves on our decision; but barely had we entered the sheet of water which separated us from our goal, when the skiff was tossed about by formidable waves.   I don't know what my friends thought, but as for me, if I had not feared to draw down upon me a lecture from Mr. M., I would have proposed to turn back.   In this, I was obeying the dictates, not of fear, but of prudence.   For if the boat had capsized, even admitting that we might have saved ourselves by swimming, we would have lost everything, and rendered it impossible to continue our journey.   We maintained absolute silence rowing vigorously, and keeping our eyes fixed on the island, where we wished to land.   In some places, the water was no more than seven feet deep, and the bottom was often visible between two consecutive waves.   The boat would disappear suddenly in the midst of the waves, to rise immediately afterwards and again disappear. Soon the wind became so violent, we were not able to go any farther; so we turned obliquely towards the left, and, in a short time, we were sailing through the tall grass, surrounding some islands, upon one of which we landed, and found that it afforded us a sure shelter, although a rapid current was running around it.

Once having pitched the tent, Mr. R. and I started in search of a channel, notwithstanding the storm, which was redoubling its violence.   Our intention was to circumnavigate the islands, hoping to find some branch of the river.   We had grounds for believing that our search would be successful on account, as I said before, of the current which we had noticed around the island on which we were encamped. But after many hours rowing among high and almost impenetrable grasses, and the sun being low in the heavens, I proposed to Mr. R. to adjourn our search till the morrow, and return to camp. To this he agreed, and we successfully rejoined our friends, who were becoming uneasy on our account.

The next day, the 3rd of July, we could neither go in search of the channel nor prepare our food in consequence of a pelting rain, and a violent wind, which continued until the afternoon of the 5th. Not expecting to remain long on the road, we had not taken any books, which in such a situation are a useful pastime. For want of books, whilst my travelling companions held discussions, I passed my time in solving mathematical problems, and this recreation was as good as any other. Mr. M., whose sonorous voice made itself heard incessantly, did not understand my indifference in such circumstances, and seeing that I held aloof from their discussions, he addressed me in the following terms.

"Here we have been for two days, able neither to advance nor recede, instead of sharing our anxieties, you do nothing but describe circles, trace planes and draw lines. To what result will that bring you? Have you found the channels we are in search of?" "I would like to know," said I, "whether with your long discussions, you are more advanced than I. As soon as the weather will permit of it, I will be the first to search for the channel."

In the afternoon of the 5th of July, the wind having ceased, as I said above, Mr. R. and I put off in the boat, and on turning the island, we perceived about half a mile before us, a narrow channel through the aquatic plants, and we resolved to take that direction the next day.

The 6th of July, at four o'clock a. m., we bid adieu to the island. The weather was magnificent, and, in a moment, having crossed the sheet of water which separated us from the high grass, we entered the channel which ran through the aquatic plants. This channel led to a rapid which conducted us into another pond which my companions wished to traverse lengthwise, while I proposed to go ahead. Happily my advice was followed, for we soon entered a branch of the river into which a great number of channels empty. It was not long before the river itself appeared, and at eight o'clock we landed at the Indian settlement, near a place where four or five half-breeds were building a warehouse for the Hudson Bay Co. We immediately went to see the Indian chief, with whom we exchanged some flour for sturgeon—and it was time to change our diet, for, during six days, we had been condemned to eat nothing but cakes baked on a tin plate in front of the fire, and butter. We tried also to get an Indian guide, but, notwithstanding our advantageous offers, no one would come with us.

After a plentiful repast, we resumed our journey, and soon entered Cedar Lake and, though it was not calm, we resolved to coast the left shore, according to our instructions. Sailing thus we reached, about two o'clock in the afternoon, the Grand Bay, where we landed on a island to dine. From there, we saw in the distance, a point of land which extended so far into the lake that it appeared to touch the right shore. We at first doubted whether it was Rabbit Point, but we soon recognised it as such by the description which had been given us. When we left the island the lake was calm, but soon a wind, coming from the Grand Bay, arose and tossed the skiff in such a manner, that, for an hour, we were in the greatest danger. Mr. R. proposed that we should go back to the island, but we refused to listen to his entreaties, fearing that, for a good many days, we might have not have finer weather, and in this we were right as the sequel will show. Notwithstanding our utmost efforts, the day was drawing to a close, and a considerable distance separated us from Rabbit Point; we therefore steered towards the point which appeared the nearest, and the sun was setting when we landed there. The place where we disembarked was not favourable for camping, as it was a narrow point of land, destitute of vegetable soil and covered with rocks. After having selected a place, we cleared it, and then erected the tent for the night. But we were not to enjoy any repose, assailed as we were by the mosquitoes, and by the waves which, in consequence of the renewal of the storm, inundated our camping ground.

Daylight came, and the storm was still raging with great fury. We held a consultation as to which of the two courses we should pursue : wait where we were for a calm, or resume our journey in order to reach Rabbit

Point from which we were separated by an hour's sail. We agreed on the last course, fearing that, if we followed the first, we might remain there blockaded for several days by the bad weather. As we were starting, we resolved to keep close to the shore, in case the boat should capsize; but, on account of the numerous small bays situated on our way, we soon perceived that, in following such a course, we would lose a great deal of time, and therefore resolved to sail before the wind, in a straight line, towards Rabbit Point. The more we advanced, the more threatening the waves became, so much so, that some of them were filling up the boat. The situation was critical, but none of us lost for a moment his "sang-froid," and, while my companions directed the boat, I baled out the water according as it poured in. After exerting our utmost efforts, we at last neared Rabbit Point; but great disappointment was awaiting us there; for, instead of the river which we expected to meet, we saw something like a prolongation of the lake where the waves were more menacing than elsewhere. We approached the Point in order to land, but we found this impossible in consequence of the rocks being on a level with the water, and through which the waves prevented us from guiding the skiff. We therefore had to turn the Point, and struggle with the waves in order to reach, a few hundred yards further on, a small bay which could afford us shelter. In this we succeeded, and pitched the tent, having resolved to await the end of the storm before resuming our journey.

According to our instructions, we should have felt the current of the river at reaching Rabbit Point, but this was far from being the case, for, as we have seen, we had to row with all our might to make any headway at all. Therefore Mr. R. was of opinion that this point was not Rabbit Point, but some point on Mossy Portage which separates Cedar Lake from Lake Winnipegoosis. For my part, I did not share his idea, and I accounted for the existence of the formidable waves we had encountered in turning the Point by the wind blowing against the current and giving, as a most striking proof, the waves with which we were assailed on turning Mosquito Point. Mr. R. ended by thinking I was right, and we all congratulated ourselves that we were not far from the end of our journey.

CHAPTER XVIII.

THE 9th of July found us encamped at Rabbit Point,
and the storm, which abated only for a short time at
night, was still raging with fury. Something had to be
done, as our provisions were almost exhausted, and the
best course to pursue we could see was to resume our
journey, if we did not wish to die of hunger. Accordingly
we set sail keeping along the left shore, as we had been
instructed, struggling manfully with the storm. We had
been travelling in that manner for an hour, when, a mile
ahead, we saw, in a birch canoe, an Indian coming towards
us. In our situation this chance meeting was a very welcome one, for we hoped to obtain from him some information, and perhaps some provisions. As soon as he was
within call, we hailed him; but whether from fear, or
some other motive, he paddled as fast as he could for the
bay, which is separated from Cedar Lake only by a half
mile portage, thus avoiding a long circuit.

After setting out from an island on which we had

dined, we came directly in sight of alluvial deposits where
the sheet of water in which we were travelling from Rabbit Point, divided in two branches. " My friends," said I,
" this alluvial soil is an incontestable proof that we are in
the bed of the river. The question is, which of the
branches we ought to take. I propose that we take the
one to the left."

" I agree with you," said Mr. R., " for, notwithstanding
the wind and the waves, it seems to me that the current
is carrying us in that direction. Moreover, in doing so,
we shall only follow our instructions."

But Mr. M. expressed a different opinion. Taking the
map, he showed us, below Cedar Lake, a small bay which
he believed to be the left branch we wanted to take.
Therefore he recommended the right branch as being the
one we should follow. As Mr. G. appeared indifferent in
the matter, the advice of Mr. M. was followed, but on
condition, that, if in two or three hours we were not sure
of being in the right way, we would return to the delta
to take the left branch.

Impelled by the wind and the oars, we sailed very
quickly and soon found ourselves among rocky islands,
most of them covered with firs, but presenting on their
shores no trace of alluvial deposits. This was an infallible proof that we were getting further and further away
from the bed of the river. I communicated my fears to
my travelling companions, but they answered that they
would keep the same direction as long as the boat would
float.

Towards evening the sky became cloudy, and the thunder began to roar in the distance ; everything foreboded a violent storm.   Our situation became still more critical when Mr. R., who was at the helm, announced that he heard the roaring of a cataract.

"It is to a certainty the Demi-Charge," said Mr. M., turning towards me, as much as to say we were in the right way.   We ceased rowing ; we thought really that we heard in the distance a dull and confused noise. Therefore we steered immediately towards the nearest island in order to land.

" What ! " exclaimed Mr. M., making a jump on his seat which almost capsized the skiff, '" after having lost more than a week among the islands of Cedar Lake and at Rabbit Point, you want, on account of the Demi-Charge, to lose another day ?   I will not consent, and I give you to understand that I will reach Grand Rapids this very night."

Without taking any notice of Mr. M.'s protestations, we continued to steer towards the island.   But what was our astonishment when, the weather clearing up, we saw we were travelling in swampy water ; evident proof that we were miles and miles away from the river.   As for the noise which led us to believe that we were approaching the Demi-Charge, we no longer heard it after the storm. As it was useless to go any farther in that direction, we started on the way back, and, at night-fall we camped on a island covered with gigantic fir trees.   Mr. R. made an observatory of the highest one, but his efforts to find out

where we stood proved unsuccessful on account of
the surrounding country being covered with trees of
higher stature.   Sleep that night was out of the question,
and how could it be otherwise, having, for provisions, only
a few pounds of flour, which, with the strictest economy,
would not last more than four days.

At half past two, next morning, we put off.   Mr. M.
very much affected by the mistake of the preceding day,
declared that, from that moment, he would not give any
advice about which way we should, or should not take.
We travelled pretty fast as long as we were sailing among
islands, but when we came to the open water, our progress was very slow, as we had the wind and the waves
to contend with; so that it was only after six hours of
hard rowing that we reached the Delta.   In leaving this
place, Mr. R. demanded the control of the boat for two
hours only, promising that if, at the end of that time,
we had not reached the Demi-Charge, he would resign his
trust to somebody else.   His demand was granted; and,
sailing along the left shore, we carefully scrutinized all the
bays which were large enough to conceal an outlet.   Before long, we arrived at the entrance of a bay delineated
on the map, having no name, but which I shall call
" Hunger Bay," in remembrance of the hunger which we
there experienced.   As the entrance of this bay was nar-
now, Mr. R. was led to believe the river was running
through it, and therefore steered the boat into it.   Always
coasting the left shore, we went to the farthest end of
the bay, but there, no outlet was found.   These fruitless

12

attempts discouraged at last Mr. R.   He declared that
he not only renounced the direction of the boat, but the
same as Mr. M. the giving of any opinion. This avowal
from the mouth of such an energetic man discouraged me
not a little, and Mr. G. refusing to take his place, this
duty devolved upon me. I therefore took the helm, and
announced that the day would be devoted to making in-
vestigations ; but that if, night having come, we had not
found the river again, we would return to the Indian
Settlement of Cedar Lake, where we would await the
arrival of the *Northcote.*

Aided by the wind, we were soon at the mouth of the
bay, whence we turned to the left, steering towards a fir
tree with its branches lopped off near the top, exactly
like the one we had seen the first day we went astray.
I had remarked similar trees on some of the islands near
Rabbit Point and in the vicinity of the Indian Settlement
at Cedar Lake.   It occurred to me that those lopped
trees indicated, perhaps, the channel followed by the
boats of the Hudson Bay Co. and I was not mistaken.
I learned it afterwards from one of the employees. The
more we advanced, the muddier the water became, a
proof that we were nearing the bed of the river.

"My friends," said I, unable to restrain my joy, "we
shall soon arrive at the   Demi-Charge." "Stop your
everlasting arrive," interrupted Mr. M., "let us rather
find out where we are."   "Come, Mr. M." said I, "we are
all four going to Winnipeg.   I offer you a wager : if, in an
hour' at the most, we have not entered the bed of the

river, on our arrival at Winnipeg, I will pay for a dinner for us four ; otherwise, you shall pay for it."

Mr. M. would doubtless have accepted my wager if he had not noticed that the current was becoming perceptible. The banks, even, were not long in showing themselves, and we soon arrived at the point where the river divides itself into two branches. According to the instructions received, we took the left, and now, what occupied our minds was the Demi-Charge which was not far off. We advanced slowly, listening to the least noise, and observing attentively the windings of the river. We were not long before we heard a dull noise in the distance, which was made by the Demi-Charge. " Let us land," said Mr. R., who was at the helm. " After having twice lost our way, here we are at last safe and sound at the end of our journey. Let us take care not to commit any more imprudent acts."

"Do you want to make this journey last forever?" exclaimed Mr. M., starting from his seat. " The rapid is not in sight, and you talk of landing ! What for, if you please ? Let us go on, we shall land soon enough."

We continued to advance. The rapid was not yet visible, but judging by the noise which was becoming more and more distinct, it could not be very distant. Mr. R. insisted upon landing, but Mr. M. obstinately refused. Mr. G. and I. remained silent, thinking it would be time enough to decide when we should be in sight of the rapid.

" If you want to run the rapid," said Mr. R. at last, "do so at your own risk, I will land."

He had hardly spoken these words, when, about 100 yards ahead, appeared the Demi-Charge, *nolens-volens* we had to advance.

"Take the helm," said Mr. R. to Mr. M., "if we meet with any misfortune, you alone will be responsible for it."

Mr. M. grew pale, but with admirable sang-froid, he took the helm exclaiming : " pull hard."   In the twinkling of an eye, we shot into the midst of boiling, raging, whirl-pools.   Sometimes the prow of the boat disappeared in the waves, sometimes the stern.   The banks also appeared and disappeared alternately.   We rowed with all our might, hardly breathing, the situation was so critical. Before us, rose a column of water several feet high.   To avoid it, we turned slightly to the left.   But not sufficient-ly to prevent a *jet d'eau* from partly filling the boat.   A little farther, this branch of the river divides into three other branches of which we took the first to the left which is followed by the boats, and is the least danger-ous.   We arrived thus at the entrance of Cross Lake, where we landed to empty the boat.   "Behold the famous Demi-Charge safely run," exclaimed Mr. M., " if you wish we will also run the Grand Rapids."

The enthusiasm of Mr. M. was far from being shared by any one of us, and especially by Mr. R. who, after we had landed, proposed that we should examine the rapid in following along the shore the footpath mentioned by the director of Pas Mission.   But the river being then high, we found this footpath overflown with the water, and, unable to proceed any farther through the bush, we returned to our landing-place.

Immediately after dinner, as we were drying our clothes in the sun, which had been wet by the *jet d'eau,* above mentioned, we saw two men coming towards us in a birch canoe. One of them was the Indian chief of the tribe at Grand Rapids. He is a man of about forty years of age, with a sharp intelligent eye, and very loquacious. The beard, which adorns his chin, shows that some white blood runs in his veins. He informed us that the *Northcote* had set out from Grand Rapids that morning, and that it would probably anchor that evening at the foot of Red Rock rapid. From where we stood he showed us in fact, on the other side of the lake, a lopped fir tree, and beyond this tree, the smoke of the steamboat. We bought some sturgeon from him, and this change of diet was most welcome, for, on dry bread, we were becoming gradually weak.

After the chief had asked us the reason why we came down the river in a rowing boat, he informed us that they were going a little farther up the river to weed some potatoes. This surprised not a little Mr. R., who had not yet recovered from his excitement, and he asked the Indian how they were going to ascend the rapids.

" In the canoe, certainly," answered the chief, surprised at this question.

" In the canoe! how ? "

" By keeping along the bank, you will see how."

In fact the Indians got into the canoe and went away, ascending the Demi-Charge, by following the sinuosities of the shore. A bark canoe permits of evolutions impossible for heavier crafts.

The next day, at five o'clock in the morning, we set out again, steering towards the lopped tree which the Indian chief had pointed out to us, on the other side of the lake. The crossing, which is only of three miles, was effected without danger ; for the lake was calm : a rare thing, because the current of the Demi-Charge crosses it completely. In fact, the wind blowing against the current is all that is necessary to produce a storm capable of swamping the largest boats. Hence the Indian chief had expressly recommended us not to set out if there was the least wind.

The river leaves the lake by many branches. We took the first to the right, and soon reached Little Red Rock Rapid, which is of little importance, and which we ran without difficulty. From there we heard the roaring of Red Rock Rapid, and a little farther down, on turning a point, we came in view of the *Northcote* which was ascending the rapid by following the right shore. There was no time to lose ; we immediately steered towards the right bank, rowing with all our might. We succeeded in effecting a landing where the hauling cable of the *Northcote* was attached. Our way of proceeding did not please, in the least, Mr. M., and he went so far as to threaten to run the rapids alone, but his threats came to nothing, as he had the majority against him.

After having been there half an hour, we noticed that

the steamboat did not appear to have stirred; we therefore held a council about what course we should pursue.
Mr. R. was of opinion that the best for us to do was to
wait there, until the *Northcote* would have ascended the
rapid. This certainly was the safest course, but, in following it, how long would we have to wait there ? Probably the whole day, and Mr. M. argued that the best
thing to do was to resume our journey. To this, we all
finally agreed, excepting Mr. R. who resigned to Mr. G.
his place at the helm, not wishing to have any share in
this mad undertaking.

Having all re-embarked, we put off, and, in a few sec-
onds, we had reached the rapid. Seen from a distance,
our skiff resembled a pigmy running to measure its
strength with a giant. Afraid of a collision with the
Northcote, we turned obliquely to the left, and by this
measure, we ran into the heart of the rapid, where we received such shocks that we forgot the preceding tossings.
The boat was carried to the summit of the waves in a
perpendicular direction, and plunged afterwards into the
abyss whence it emerged to mount the next wave. The
banks of the river appeared and disappeared in turns, and
we shot by the steamer like an arrow, at a distance of
about three hundred feet from her. The passengers, quite
surprised to see four men resembling brigands, descend
the rapids in such a frail bark, began to speculate as to
the result of our undertaking. Some urged that we were
going to founder, but most of them had hopes of our final
success.

Having arrived at the foot of the rapid, we perceived, on the left bank, the Fort of the Hudson Bay Company, which is situated above the Grand Rapids. The wharf of the *Northcote* is located here, and here ended our adventurous prank.

As soon as we landed, the director of the establishment came towards us, thinking that we were part of the crew of the *Northcote*, and that we were the bearers of news from the boat. But he soon discovered his mistake. Our tattered clothes and worn out shoes gave us the appearance of four desperadoes who wanted to take possession of the Fort. This was, I think, the opinion of the director, judging by the frightened glances which he cast towards the houses of the Company's employees, as if to implore assistance. We soon reassured him by telling him that he should not judge by appearances, and that all we wanted was to buy some provisions.

The news of our arrival spread rapidly, and in the evening, an Indian sold us a sturgeon which weighed sixty pounds. He was accompanied too, by several squaws, from whom we purchased a quantity of strawberries which they had gathered in the neighbourhood. Our diet was thus changed as if by enchantment, and we soon forgot our recent privations and fatigues.

But for our delay at Rabbit Point, we should have arrived in time to take the *Colville*, which had gone to Stone Fort three days before. Before returning to Grand Rapids, she had to make a voyage to Norway House, a Hudson Bay Fort situated on Nelson River. This voyage

requires at least a week; consequently we were obliged
to remain about ten days at Grand Rapids. Mr. M. suggested that we should proceed to Winnipeg with the boat
in which we had displayed our prowess and *madness*, but
the rest of us took good care not to undertake this foolish
project

The Grand Rapids, which flow between two calcareous
banks, are a mile and a half long, and but for the rocks,
on a level with the water, which encumber the bed of the
river, the boats could ascend them in the same manner as
the other rapids. At the foot of these rapids, on the left
bank of the river, a mile above its mouth, there is a Hudson Bay Company's Fort, the landing place of the *Colville* ;
and on the opposite bank, an Indian settlement which extends along the river from the Grand Rapids to Lake
Winnipeg. The inhabitants, except a few who are in the
service of the Hudson Bay Company, live by hunting and
fishing, the only means of subsistence which they have at
their command, for this region is essentially rocky, and is
unfit for the cultivation of cereals.

Recently the Hudson Bay Company has had a tramway
built, connecting the wharves of the *Colville* and the
Northcote ; and it is by means of this tramway, that
transhipment of merchandise brought by the *Colville*,
and intended for the North-West, is effected; a process
more rapid, and less fatiguing than that formerly employed
by travellers, who themselves carried their luggage a distance of a mile and a half.

It is only in July that the *Northcote* can set out and

this delay arises from two causes, the late breaking up of the ice in Lake Winnipeg, and the insufficiency of the tonnage of the *Colville*, which to load the *Northcote*, has to make three voyages, each of which takes a week. The second cause of delay would be easily obviated, by launching on Lake Winnipeg a boat of the same tonnage as the *Northcote*, or several boats like the *Colville*. In supposing that this should be realized, the *Northcote* would not be ready to leave Grand Rapids before the first of July, on account of Lake Winnipeg being not free of ice, until about the middle of June. Therefore, notwithstanding the best previsions, a journey from Winnipeg to Edmonton, *via* Grand Rapids could not be effected before the latter end of July. In the interests of colonization, could there not be another way opened, other than the inconvenient one, *via* Grand Rapids ? There certainly could, and it only remains to utilize it ; I mean the route, *via* the Lakes Winnipegoosis and Manitoba.

The southern end of Lake Manitoba is about fifty miles from Winnipeg, and this lake is connected with Lake Winnipegoosis whose northern end is separated from Cedar Lake by Mossy Portage which is only about five miles long. With a railway from Winnipeg to Lake Manitoba, steamboats on the Lakes Manitoba and Winnipegoosis, a railway or canal through Mossy Portage, and steamboats on the Saskatchewan, one could rapidly reach the North-West, thus avoiding the dangerous rapids between Cedar Lake and Winnipeg. I say dangerous, especially in ascending them ; for if the tow cables break, there is nothing to prevent the boats from being wrecked against the rocks along the shore : as witness the catastrophe which befel the *Commissioner* belonging to the Hudson Bay Co., in 1873. This was the first steamboat that appeared on the waters of the Saskatchewan, and, on her first voyage, as she was ascending the Demi-Charge, the tow cables broke, an,d in a second, the *Commissioner* was broken in pieces against the rocks. Happily, the crew succeeded in saving themselves.

Though the route, *via* Lakes Manitoba and Winnipegoosis, would be the best for colonists who wish to reach the far North-West, we do not mean to say that the route by Grand Rapids should be abandoned. On the contrary, when the projected railway, connecting Hudson Bay will be built, this will be the most economical and the most direct way of exporting to Europe the grain from the Saskatchewan valley. The above is a project which the government would do well to carry into execution.

Our stay at Grand Rapids appeared very long to us. We passed our time in fishing and picking strawberries. Fish are plentiful at the foot of the rapids. In a quarter of an hour, one can catch with a hook and line, more fish than he can carry. Strawberries are no less plentiful ; and I have often asked myself, if this region, though rocky, might not be appropriated advantageously to the cultivation of fruit. One would easily believe it, if one considers that here the summer is pretty warm, and during that season, night frosts are very rare, on account of the composition of the soil, and the proximity of Lake Winnipeg. Let us hope that our statesmen will take into consideration a question so directly concerning the future of the country.

CHAPTER XIX.

Departure from Grand Rapids—Icelandic Settlement on Lake Winnipeg—Selkirk—Our Arrival at Winnipeg—Rapid Progress of that Place since 1870—*En route* for Ontario—Ideas of Americans about Canada—Duluth—Good Pastime on the Lakes—Visiting my Friends Once More—My Arrival at Quebec and on board of the *Sarmatian*, *en route* for Liverpool.

AFTER a week passèd above the Grand Rapids, we took the tramway for the wharf of the *Colville* where, with the leave of the director of the Fort, we installed ourselves in the warehouse which is used to receive the cargo of the steamboat. These camping quarters were far more comfortable than that of Mr. R., which could hardly shelter us from the abundant showers of rain, so frequent, in that region, at that season of the year, Our stay there was not to be long, for, on the night of the 28th, we were awakened by the director calling out that the *Colville* was in sight. Hardly had we got up and took out our baggage, when the steamer anchored, and the unloading immediately began. This was completed the next morning at 11 o'clock and at 10 that night, we weighed anchor, the Indians giving us a parting salute from their guns, to which the Captain replied by a whistle from the engine. This seemed to please them greatly, if one can judge by their shouts which they continued as long as we remained in view.

Being then only July, a cool night had succeeded the tropical heat of the day. Not the least breath rippled the surface of the lake, and the boat seemed to glide upon a vast mirror. But from this, it must not be inferred, that Lake Winnipeg is always calm; for violent storms sometimes arise which expose boats to the greatest dangers; and are increased by the shallowness of the lake and the presence of rocky islands. Before retiring for the night, I approached the Captain and asked him how long it would take us to reach Stone Fort.

"If the fine weather continues" said he, "we shall be there in thirty-six hours, that is to say, about ten o'clock Saturday morning." This answer was all the more agreeable to us, since we wanted to reach Winnipeg by Saturday evening if possible.

The cabins of the *Colville* which, like those of the *Lily*, contained each two beds, were not very comfortable; but we were better off with respect to board. As for the crew, it was composed principally of Indians and half-breeds speaking, I think, all the Indian dialects of Canada.

The next day in the afternoon, we arrived in sight of Icelandic Settlement, which has been founded since 1875, upon the southern shore of Lake Winnipeg. One asks oneself with surprise, what those colonists were thinking of to settle in such a place; for that part of the country, taken on the whole, is unsuitable for the culture of cereals. It would have been better for them to settle elsewhere, and cultivate the soil on a large scale, than to get a precarious living by fishing in Lake Winnipeg, and cultivating a few rows of potatoes. Saturday, at daybreak we arrived at the mouth of Red River where we met the pilot who was to take charge of the *Colville* as far as the Stone Fort, I must say here, that the current of Red River is not so swift as that of the Saskatchewan; but its channel is much more sinuous, hence it is very hard to follow it when the water is muddy. Such was the case then, and at one time, the pilot having swerved from the channel, the trunk of a tree got entangled in the screw, and stopped the boat. No harm was done, however, to the machinery of the *Colville*, which soon resumed its course. As for the pilot, all he had to endure was a few objurgations from the chief engineer. We were not long before we came in sight of Selkirk, where we landed at eight o'clock that morning.

We did not go to the Stone Fort with the *Colville*, as we expected, having heard that we could reach Winnipeg sooner by taking at Selkirk the morning train which leaves for St. Boniface. Unfortunately after we had landed, we learned that the train we intended to take had already left, and there being no other train that day, which we could take, we hired a carriage to take us to Winnipeg in the afternoon.

Selkirk, which is of very recent origin, had made prodigious progress. The reason of this may be partly attributed to the supposition that the Canadian Pacific Railway, now under construction, was to pass through that

town.   Selkirk contains hotels which would do honour
to Ontario or Quebec ; and publishes a weekly newspaper
called the *Inter-Ocean*.   The prospects are that this town,
connected with Winnipeg by railway, situated on Red
River, and being in the centre of a very fertile district,
is destined to become a place of importance.   .

At three o'clock in the afternoon, we set out for Winnipeg, eighteen miles distant.   The road we followed lies along
Red River and passes through Stone Fort, St. Andrews,
and Kildonan.   Stone Fort comprises hardly anything but
the Hudson Bay establishment.   As for St. Andrews and
Kildonan, they are prosperous, and rapidly growing.   As
it was at the season of the year when the weather was
fine, and nature was clothed in all its beauty, our drive was
very agreeable, and we entered Winnipeg charmed with
the splendid panorama which, since leaving Selkirk, had
unrolled itself to our view.   Mr. G. alighted at the house
of his relatives, Messrs. R. and M., and I took lodgings at
the Hotel du Canada.

Winnipeg, the capital of Manitoba, has a population of
about sixteen thousand souls, and is situated at the junction of the Assiniboine and Red Rivers.   This city, which
was but a small village in 1870, has grown even more
rapidly than Chicago, the metropolis of the North-Western
States.

To give the reader an idea of the progress made by that
place since 1870, let us picture to ourselves the impres-
sions of an inhabitant of Winnipeg, who, at that time, had
gone to a foreign land, and is returning to-day to his na-

tive country. If he be in Canada or in the United States, he takes a ticket for St. Boniface, situated opposite Winnipeg. Arrived at St. Vincent, he leaves the United States to enter Manitoba. A thousand reminiscences crowd into his mind at the sight of the vast plains on which he had many a time hunted the buffalo. But what impresses and grieves him, are the changes which have taken place in those parts. Domesticated cattle have succeeded the buffaloes which have entirely disappeared ; the virgin plains, under the effort of settlers, have been partly converted into cultivated fields; wigwams and cabins have given place to elegant houses. Judge of the disappointment of our Manitoban ! The farther he advances, the more he is pained by the changes that have taken place. Finally the train stops, and they call out : "St. Boniface—Winnipeg." He alights from the car, and looks around; but the dwellings he beholds resemble in no wise the cabins of former days. The church alone, where he attended mass, and which has undergone no change, proves to him that he is at the end of his journey. Mechanically, he follows his fellow-travellers, and, with them, takes the omnibus which crosses Red River, on a steam-ferry. They pass before the principal hotels of Winnipeg ; the omnibus gradually gets rid of the passengers. Our Manitoban, finally left alone, asks to be driven to his home ; but the omnibus conductor, who however is thoroughly acquainted with the city, declares that he does not know his address. This answer surprises a great deal our traveller. He asks then to be taken to Fort Garry where, in former days, he

13

used to sell his furs to the Hudson Bay Company. This establishment has so well resisted the hand of progress that our traveller finds at last where he is, and the place where he was born. But his father's home is no more, and on its place is perhaps erected a magnificent building. His discovery only adds to his regrets. His old friends are dead or have emigrated to wild lands ; the steamboats have replaced the canoes on Red River ; broad streets have succeeded the narrow cart roads ; and houses, which would do honour to a great city, the Indian wigwams and the log cabins of the half-breeds. All this is what has been done in ten years ! What will be done in ten more?

After passing three days in Winnipeg, I started for Ontario with Mr. M., who was still determined to make his trans-Atlantic voyage. Mr. G. remained at Winnipeg, and Mr. R. was to return to Battleford.

In summer, one can go from Winnipeg to Ontario by two different routes; the first and most expeditious by rail, *via* St. Paul, Chicago and Sarnia; the second, by rail, from St. Boniface to Duluth, and from there by steamboat, several of which ply between Duluth and Sarnia, In summer it is more agreeable to travel by boat than by rail ; and for this reason and also because I desired to see Lakes Superior and Huron, I chose the second.

On the 3rd of August, at seven o'clock a. m., we left St. Boniface, and, in the afternoon, we entered the plains of Minnesota. This country, sparsely populated in 1874, is to-day almost completely colonized. Along the railway, between St. Boniface and Duluth, one sees villages and flourishing towns, of which the principal are :—St. Vincent, Brookston, Glyndon, and Brainerd.

The Americans imagine that their country is superior to all others. Among my fellow-travellers, one could easily distinguish between the Americans, and others. The former could not contain their admiration at the sight of the rich fields of wheat which extended along the railroad. A traveller, seated opposite to me, seeing that I did not share in his enthusiasm, asked me if I knew a country comparable to this :

"I know one," said I, "which is much superior." "Superior !" said he, "not in America, any way." "Yes, in America," said I, "and in Canada, too." "I would like to know which Province of Canada is more fertile than Minnesota ?" "It is not a province," said I, "but a region scarcely yet known. I mean the upper part of the North Saskatchewan Valley."

It is evident the fertility of Minnesota is incomparable in the eyes of him who has not visited the Canadian North-West, Hence my indifference at the sight of a country which had excited the admiration of the travellers. They listened with a lively interest to all the details that I gave about the Saskatchewan region, the natural richness of which was only partially known. They did not understand how the Canadian Government had left such a vast and fertile country so long in the hands of fur-traders. Thus, unintentionally, I was performing the functions of an emigration agent, for several of the m seem disposed to sell their land in order to go to the Canadian North-West.

The following day, at noon, the train entered Duluth. On our arrival, omnibuses conveyed the travellers, going to Ontario, to the *Quebec*. This steamer was going to start at night-fall, and, as I then had several hours before me, I went after dinner to visit Duluth and its vicinity. Situated at the head of a bay called Fond du Lac, this city extends along the shore, and is backed by rocky, inaccessible hills, which prevent it from developing in that direction. Its longitudinal streets, disposed like an amphitheatre, are well supplied with comfortable hotels. Duluth is still prosperous, though its former prosperity is somewhat diminished in consequence of the openings of railway connection between Ontario and the North-West. But that which will mark its decline, more particularly, will be the completion of the railroad from Thunder Bay to Manitoba, and which will be followed by travellers going from Ontario to the North-West.

Towards evening I returned on board of the *Quebec* which soon weighed anchor. All those who have travelled on the boats of Lake Superior have been greatly pleased with the comfort of them. Each cabin contains two berths; but they are much more roomy than those of the Saskatchewan steamboats.

The passengers, most of whom were tourists, were not very numerous. The feminine sex was chiefly represented by some American misses, who, from the first day, enlivened the company, by playing captivating pieces on the piano. The musical faculty, which had been slumbering in me for six years, suddenly awoke on hearing these harmonious strains. What a contrast between the music and the deafening uproar produced by the tambourine of the savages. The latter I endured with difficulty; the former I heard with pleasure. The one grated upon my ear; the other excited my imagination, and awoke in me a world of ideas and sentiments which I was not before aware of. There is in music, even in secular music, something that elevates the soul and awakens in it the sense of the Infinite. By music, as by poetry, we reach the invisible, the immutable, the eternal. I almost reproached myself for my voluntary exile among the Indians who afforded so little attraction for any man accustomed to society. But without this isolation I should not have gained that experience, and made observations which I hope one day to make known to the public. Like those bold travellers who, for a purely scientific object, leave family, native land, and the advantages of civilization, to encounter unexpected and inevitable dangers, I have resolved, after a study of the North-West of Canada, to relate some day its natural riches, which are to-day being taken advantage of by thousands of colonists.

The third day we reached Sault Ste. Marie Rapid, which separates Lake Superior from Lake Huron. To avoid it a canal has been built through which the boats pass. The next day, in the evening, we reached Sarnia. There I parted with Mr. M. whom I arranged to meet in Toronto. By the Grand Trunk I went to London, where

I visited some friends whom I had not seen since 1873.
Three days later I started for Toronto.   Mr. M. was not
at the rendezvous, and my endeavours to find him were
fruitless.   So, after visiting Niagara, I set out for Quebec,
(passing by Ottawa and Montreal), where I arrived just
in time to sail for Liverpool by the *Sarmatian.*

Here ends the account of my adventures in the North-
West.